muniya's light

With all good wishes
Rambara Yadav

OTHER INDIAINK TITLES :

Anjana Appachana	*Listening Now*
I. Allan Sealy	*The Everest Hotel*
I. Allan Sealy	*Trotternama*
Indrajit Hazra	*The Garden of Earthly Delights*
Manju Kapur	*A Married Woman*
Marina Budhos	*The Professor of Light*
Pankaj Mishra	*The Romantics*
Paro Anand	*I'm Not Butter Chicken*
Paro Anand	*No Guns at My Son's Funeral*
Paro Anand	*Wingless*
Ranjit Lal	*The Life &Times of Altu-Faltu*
Susan Visvanathan	*Something Barely Remembered*
Susan Visvanathan	*The Visiting Moon*

FORTHCOMING TITLES :

Ranjit Lal	*The Small Tigers of Shergarh*
Tom Alter	*The Longest Race*
Sharmistha Mohanty	*New Life*
Kalpana Swaminathan	*The Page 3 Murders*
C. P. Surendran	*An Iron Harvest*

muniya's light
a narrative of truth and myth

ramchandra gandhi

IndiaInk
ROLI BOOKS

IndiaInk

© Ramchandra Gandhi 2005
All rights reserved. No part of this publication may be
reproduced or transmitted, in any form or by any means,
without the prior permission of the publisher.

This edition first published in 2005
IndiaInk
An imprint of Roli Books Pvt. Ltd.
M-75, G.K. II Market, New Delhi 110 048
Phones: ++91 (011) 2921 2271, 2921 2782
2921 0886, Fax: ++91 (011) 2921 7185
E-mail: roli@vsnl.com; Website: rolibooks.com
Also at Bangalore, Varanasi, Jaipur and the Netherlands

Cover design: Arati Subramanyam
Layout design: Kumar Raman
Cover photograph: K.S. Radhakrishnan, Pradeep Das Gupta and Art
Alive Gallery, New Delhi

Picture credits: Pgs. 5, 31, 37, Ramana Kendra, New Delhi; Pg. 51,
Samata Books, Chennai; Pg. 63, Tyeb Mehta and Suresh & Saroj
Bhayana Family Collection; Pg. 93, Tyeb Mehta; Pgs. 101, 215,
Ramakrishna Mission, New Delhi; Pg. 111, The Munch
Museum/The Munch-Ellingsen Group/Bono 2004; Pg. 115, K.S.
Radhakrishnan, Pradeep Das Gupta and Art Alive Gallery, New
Delhi; Pg. 129, Vikas Publishing House, New Delhi (*Amrita Shergil:
A Biography* by N. Iqbal Singh) and National Gallery of Modern
Art, New Delhi; Pg. 155, Gandhi Smriti, New Delhi; Pg. 179, St
Mary's Church, Oxford; Pg. 221, Tyeb Mehta and Vadehra Art
Gallery, New Delhi; Pg. 233, The Samuel Courtauld Trust,
Courtauld Institute of Art Gallery, London; Pg. 239, Aryan Books
International, New Delhi (*Symbolism in Hindu Architecture* by
L. Peter Kohlar).

ISBN: 81-86939-18-0

Typeset in Photina MT by Roli Books Pvt. Ltd. and
printed at Anubha Printers, Noida, UP.

Contents

ACKNOWLEDGEMENTS vi

REUNION 1
  Storytelling In San Francisco 3
  Airborne 19

REMEMBRANCE 23
  Beginnings 25
  Thanksgiving 30
  Miracle In Pune 40
  Birthday 42
  Jnaneshvari 49
  Iconography 62
  Indian Indivisibility 73
  Kabaddi 83
  Temptation 89
  Wanderings 92

REALITY 107
  Muniya's Anguish 109
  Lullaby 117
  Terror 122
  In London With Haren Desai 125
  Francis Bacon's Intervention 139

'Hinduism And Violence': A Lecture At The Bharatiya Vidya Bhavan	143
The Wisdom Of Hissing	149
Was Gandhi A Fraud?	153
Violence And The Girl-Child	161
Post-Pacifist Non-Violence	167
The Third Atom Bomb	171
Untouchability And The Mandukya Upanishad	175
Sankeertana In Oxford	181
Confession	183
Last Meal With The Desais	189
Conception	193
'I Want To Be Free!'	199
Grounded In Mumbai	203
Muniya's Light	206
Jnaneshvari's Consolation	209
Roles Reversed!	211
Could Ramakrishna Have Been Gay?	213
A Falling Figure	219
The Ocean's Invitation	225
Hindutva Or Sindhutva?	228
Samadhi	235
GLOSSARY	243

Acknowledgements

For many years I have had the desire to explore the significance of Hindu philosophical thought, especially Advaita Vedanta, fictionally and philosophically, with special focus on the status of the girl-child in the light of Advaita.

Muniya's Light is an attempt to do some of these things. It is an imaginary conversation between an old Indian philosopher and spiritual seeker and a young Indian woman graduate.

Travelling in space from San Francisco to Mumbai, with a brief halt in London, Ravi Srivastava (the philosopher) and Ananya Kulkarni (the young woman graduate to whom Ravi gives the name 'Muniya') travel backwards in time to the luminous years of Sri Ramakrishna's life in the late nineteenth century, and to Sri Ramana Maharshi's presence in our midst till 1950. Against the backdrop of India's struggle for svaraj and the vivisection of India and the martyrdom of Mahatma Gandhi. To make sense of darkness of our times; and of one another.

The characters and events of the narrative partake of both truth and myth, fact and fantasy, in the permissive but revelatory spirit of pauranika storytelling, and inevitably with the aid of stories from the Ramayana and the Mahabharata.

Special thanks to Indira Vancheswer for typing and retyping my manuscript with patience and encouragement; and to Jehanara Wasi for editing it with sensitivity; and to the India International Centre Library for research facilities; and, to Lalit Mohan Sharma for computerising the images reproduced in this book.

And to Sherna Wadia for her insightful help in retyping portions of the text so as to make them more reader-friendly.

Without the stimulus of conversation provided by the members of my ongoing workshop on the Bhagavadgita, bless them, this work would be even more imperfect than it is.

Fellowship grants from the Indic Studies Project of the Centre for the Study of Developing Societies and SAMUHA sustained me during lean months. I am grateful to these institutions. And to Roli Books for agreeing to publish this book.

Chhoti, Maya Singh, a friend's daughter, is now an articulate adult. But even at the age of four, like Muniya, she would not speak at all. It is possible that my imploring Chhoti to chant the sacred syllable 'Aum' may have encouraged her to break her vow of silence.

And Anjali Sen, who smiles like Muniya, and is economical but resolute in speech like her, would not let me plead old age as an excuse for not completing the project of this exploration of truth and myth.

This book is dedicated to Chhoti and Anjali, and seeks to celebrate the girl-child in all stages of her life.

Aum Sri Ramanaya Namah
Ramchandra Gandhi

New Delhi
January 2005

Reunion

May we be protected, nourished, empowered,
and enlightened together.
May we not be jealous of one another
(KATHA UPANISHAD, PEACE CHANT)

Storytelling In San Francisco

In August 2002 Ravi Srivastava was invited to conduct four workshops, one each week, at the California Institute of Integral Studies (CIIS) in San Francisco, on the theme 'War or Peace?'. The Institute expected that Professor Srivastava, a well-known interpreter of modern Indian sages and Vedanta, would be able to shed some non-mainstream, non-western light on the collapse of trust between civilisations and the widening gulf between secular modernity and religious traditions which had, a year earlier, brought about the devastating assault on the twin towers in New York by aeroplanes hijacked by terrorists.

Ravi returned to his studio apartment on Cole Street late in the evening after the end of the third workshop. The workshop, like the first two, was well attended by a cross-section of CIIS students and members of the general public.

After a quick shower and change of clothes, Ravi left the apartment and boarded a bus that took him to Geary and Masonic junction, where he got off. Crossing the road with ease (San Francisco motorists respect traffic lights) Ravi entered his local pub, which was uncomplicatedly called 'The Pub'. His favourite uncushioned chair was unoccupied, and he lowered his rheumatic frame into it with gratitude to his guru, Sri Ramana Maharshi.

Anna, a student who worked as a waitress at 'The Pub' in the evenings to pay her way through drama school, often found snatches of free time to chat with Ravi. She brought him his pint of dark English draught beer, after inserting a quarter into the pub jukebox to play Ravi's favourite Louis Armstrong song: 'What a wonderful world!'

'How did the lecture go today?' Anna asked Ravi, but she had to hurry away to serve another customer before Ravi could reply.

Offering a large first sip of the brew in his mind to Sri Ramana, Ravi reflected on the course the workshops had taken. He was particularly happy that the penultimate workshop had been almost entirely devoted to an exploration of a parable of Ramana's.

It was a parable about a king who had conquered the entire world and was afraid of nothing except his own shadow, and how he foolishly tried to bury his shadow by digging a deep pit for it and filling it, only to find the shadow staring him in the face again.

Anna found a minute to stand near Ravi again and hear the story with excitement, as her repertory was rehearsing another 'burial' story, Sophocle's *Antigone*.

'What did the king do then, Ravi?' she asked in a hurry.

'Ramana doesn't reveal what the king did then, but he tells us what we should do if our "shadow" bothers us, something we have repressed deeply in our minds and hearts, hated and feared, and wanted to be rid of, but which surfaces in our dreams to torment us, and constrains us to act in ways which hurt others and ourselves.

'We should turn towards the sun of truth, Ramana says, the truth of self-awareness, and the shadow will be behind us. Self-awareness is the core of our being, our awareness of ourselves as ourselves, reality, not some favoured form as opposed to others. Relocating ourselves at the core of our being, we spontaneously act towards "others" as we would expect them to act towards us,' Ravi explained.

Sri Ramana Maharshi

A descendant of Jewish concentration camp victims, Anna was moved by the story.

'I'll think about the parable tonight and hope to talk to you more about its message tomorrow,' she said, and disappeared to take orders from a group of people who had just occupied another table.

As Ravi left the pub after a second pint and a dinner of vegetable sandwiches, he asked Anna which was easier to remember, the lines of a play or pub orders.

'Lines, any day, Ravi, have a good night,' said Anna.

San Francisco streets go up and down and bus journeys on them, like fairground rides on giant wheels, are conducive for urgent contemplation.

Ravi wondered if, during the first two workshops, he had been wise in accepting Professor Jim Ryan's challenge (Jim, a scholar of Sanskrit and Tamil, had chaired all three workshops) that he summarise the message of the Mahabharata with only two stories from the epic: the first from its prefatory portions and the second from its concluding section. Should he not have told a third story?

In the first story, which Ravi thought was a prophetic warning to humanity of the dangers of exclusivist self-identities, Devavrata, known as Bhishma later in the epic (who took the awesome vow of brahmacharya, life-long celibacy), shoots an incarcerating ring of arrows into the ceaseless flow of self-awareness, the river Ganga, his mother.

Ravi had maintained that right there, in attempting to reduce selfhood to a given, racial form, the Kuru identity of the Kauravas and the Pandavas, Bhishma had ranged himself and the Kauravas against all other human and non-human life and nature and nothingness, all apparent 'not-self': he had planted a time-bomb of annihilation at the heart of egocentric consciousness.

Not only contemporary religious and secular exclusivist identities, even human species-identity, the idea that 'we' are the human species, all else being not-self, was such a time-bomb, Ravi had stressed, and not only that.

Even the idea that we are 'something', as opposed to nothingness, was such an invitation to all-out war.

Self and emptiness, purna and shunya, were inseparable. Poverty and prosperity, have-nots and haves (metaphors of shunya and purna) cannot be regarded as being separate from one another.

Vedanta and Buddhism and all non-dualist traditions of spirituality must supplement the ethical impulse of secularism at its best with ecological wisdom and existential urgency, if 9/11 was not to become a prelude to limitless destruction.

The second Mahabharata story which Ravi drew attention to, summarising the essence of the epic, was the mocking of generativity by Yadava youths (Krishna's kinsmen) years after the great war, when they dressed a young man in a sari, making 'her' look pregnant and asked a group of sages if they could predict the gender of the child the 'woman' was going to bring into the world.

Ravi read this episode not as an expression of cross-dressing humour, which is harmless enough, nor as gay irony, but as indicative of a desire for the holy assurance of male progeny, a prejudice which today encourages parents to abort female foetuses and threatens dangerously to diminish the female population in parts of India.

'Exclusivist identity and gender injustice will destroy the secular and spiritual foundations of life,' Ravi had warned.

Stunned silence had greeted this summary and reading of the Mahabharata. Jim Ryan and others had sounded supportive, but he could detect an underlying note of disappointment and dread in their ritual appreciation of his efforts.

The third workshop identified Sri Ramakrishna and Sri Ramana, Swami Vivekananda and Sri Aurobindo and Mahatma Gandhi as inaugurating a possibly mutational change not only in the self-understanding of Hinduism, but of humanity as a whole.

And, invoking the storyteller's license to introduce clarifying changes in sacred stories, Ravi retold a story Svami Vivekananda had narrated at the Parliament of World Religions in Chicago in 1893: a story of two frogs, a frog who lived in a well, and thought his well was the whole world, and a frog who lived on the edge of an ocean and dropped by to say hello to the frog in the well.

Svami Vivekananda's version of the story (he had heard it from none other than Sri Ramakrishna) had the frog of the well order the frog of the ocean out of his well, on the ground that no habitat of a frog, be it an ocean, could be bigger than his little well.

Vivekananda was rightly drawing attention to the banishing impatience with which narrow religious orthodoxy regarded a more inclusive spiritual perspective than its own.

Ravi made the frog of the ocean appreciate the beauty, not the bigotry, of the self-contained life of the frog of the well, the autonomy of self-restrained, local, life; and had him say this, as he bid farewell to the frog in the well:

'I have seen wells smaller than yours, brother, and oceans bigger than mine. But so long as the infinite light of the sky above them was reflected by all wells and oceans, however small or large, they are equally worthy of adoration.'

'The small and the large in today's struggle between the local and the global needed to be brought into partnership,' Ravi concluded.

Ravi could feel the relief of his audience after the apocalyptic anxiety generated during the first two workshops.

Jim's strong handshake had a sense of nervous gratitude to it.

Ravi decided to stop worrying about these matters. He had come to provoke thought, not encourage complacency, he reminded himself, as he got off at his Cole Street stop and walked slowly back to his apartment.

A glass of cold milk promised sound sleep, and Ravi was soon ready to crash on his floor mattress. But he first faced the photograph of Sri Ramana Maharshi that hung on the wall in front of him and chanted with devotional gratitude and fervour the mantra 'Aum Sri Ramanaya Namah'.

However, before he could lay himself down to sleep, the telephone rang. Inclined though he was to let it ring itself out, Ravi was pulled towards it by an irresistible force and he picked up the receiver.

'Ravi Srivastava here, who might you be?' he asked.

There was a moment of embarrassed silence. And then he heard a voice from the past, the voice of his college friend Arun Kulkarni. He had been in touch with him occasionally on the phone, since his visit to the Kulkarni home in Pune in 1984, and briefly again in 1987, but for whom and his family Ravi had boundless love.

Apologising for calling at that late hour, and only after Ravi assured him that he was not being disturbed at all, did Arun explain the purpose of his long-distance call from Pune.

'Ravi, we have not been in touch for a while. Trust you are in good health and spirits. Archana is well. Abhinava, our son, will graduate in English literature this year from St Stephen's College in Delhi.

'And Ananya, our daughter, or "Muniya" as you have always called her, and who calls you "Babu", would be graduating any day in "Art and Religion from Santa Barbara".'

'Ravi, Ananya sounded quite troubled when Archana and I spoke to her on the phone a few days ago. You might remember that she has always been a strong-willed child given to protracted spells of speechlessness. She is in a similar state right now. Can you do us a big favour?

'This is her telephone number. Would you call her and ask her if she would be willing to travel back to India with you? You don't have to say that Archana or I have asked you to bring her back home safely. You know she can throw a tantrum and go off instead to Mexico or Alaska!

'But do call her, Ravi, and allay our anxiety. She has always been very fond of you. You played a special part in her growing up.

In 1984, when you visited us from Tiruvannamalai your prayers awakened the dormant shakti of speech in her.

'She had not uttered a complete sentence for four years. You helped her chant the sacred syllable "Aum" with you and brought joy to all of us. Do call her and let me know what she thinks of the idea of travelling back home with her Babu. Here is my number. Good night, Ravi. Call me soon,' thus ended Arun's call.

Babu couldn't believe that his beloved Muniya, whom he hadn't seen for years, was on the west coast.

He took out a clean sheet of paper from his notebook and wrote on its head the mantra of obeisance 'Appa!' (that is how he addressed Sadguru Sri Ramana in his heart's sadhana) and immediately below that sacred sign he wrote 'Muniya'. And beneath that, her telephone number.

A bay foghorn blew clear notes of initiation, sounds of joy and sadness, meeting and parting.

It was an answering machine that responded to Ravi's early morning call to Muniya.

'This is Ananya, sorry I can't take your call right now. Leave a message after the beep and I'll call you back,' said the recorded voice, which was self-confessedly Muniya's.

And when the 'beep' sounded a few sinking heartbeats later, Ravi quickly but clearly said this to the machine:

'This is Babu, Muniya (do you remember me?), calling from San Francisco. I happened to speak to your Baba last night and learned from him that you might be returning home soon after graduation. So am I, after four weeks of teaching here at the California Institute of Integral Studies, with a short break in journey in London.

'Would you like us to fly back home together? My San Francisco-London flight leaves on September 11 at 7 p.m. I have an Indian travel agent friend here who can, I am sure, book you on the same flight. Baba can reimburse the cost of your flight to him later. Can you please call me at 9 p.m. tonight at the following number (Ravi spelt out the number of his pub)?'

Ravi had last and very briefly spoken to Muniya four years earlier, when she had graduated from Lady Sri Ram College in Delhi in History, and last seen her in 1987, when she was seven years old.

Her recorded voice had the authority and clarity and speed of a twenty-two-year-old graduate student. Ravi could imagine the process of maturation of that voice: from the babbling chant of 'Aum, Ayi, Baba, Babu (a name she had given him in an impish, vanishing moment of abandonment of her vow of silence), Chanti, Chanti, Chanti' with which she had ended her mouna at age four, through the schoolgirl modifications of the sound of that childish voice to the signature-specificity of a college girl, all the way to its present, impatient, adult vitality.

Ravi had never forgotten 'Muniya' (a name he had given her, a common eastern Uttar Pradesh name for a little girl and also of the Divine Mother conceived as a bird). Embedded in the name was the idea of a 'muni', the silent sage, which is how Ravi had comfortingly urged her parents, Arun and Archana, to regard her when they wrote to him worryingly about her stubborn speechlessness.

What had led Ravi to think of Ananya as a special child and person was her smile whose luminosity was eloquent in a way speech never is. A quick widening of both eyes and a simultaneous, slight, sideward, rightward movement of her closed mouth. This, Ravi thought, endorsed Ramana Maharshi's teaching that our true heart, seat of selfhood, Atman, was on the right side of our chest where there is nothing, a nothingness which was continuous with the limitless not-thingness of self-awareness or emptiness.

Ravi had failed to find that smile of grace on the face of any of the many gifted and attractive women he had had the privilege of knowing. To this failure he attributed his inability to enter into an enduring relationship with any woman.

And one reason, if not 'the' reason, why he did not visit the Kulkarni home after 1987, was his fear that Muniya may have lost that smile.

But he was able to recreate that smile on his own ageing face, and when he looked at himself in the mirror, he felt her face-to-face presence, a deep metaphor of self-awareness.

Before shaving and starting a new day, Ravi remembered that miracle as he stood before the mirror that morning in San Francisco, and walked the short distance to CIIS on Ashbury Street to conclude a discussion (the fourth workshop) with a group of feminist students at 11 a.m.

'Ravi (American students address their teachers by their first names, a democratic practice Babu entirely approved of), may I make a special request?' asked the leader of the group, Debbie. 'Could you tell us a story from the Mahabharata which reveals a free-spirited woman's attitude towards her own pregnancy, uncoerced by the expectations of patriarchy?'

This is providential, this opportunity to explore the meaning of a third story from the Mahabharata, Ravi thought.

'I think I could do that, Debbie, with the storyteller's ancient license to modify the details of a sacred story to highlight its spirit.

'May the following Mahabharata story about a woman's untutored response to her pregnancy awaken us to reality.

'After the victory of the Pandavas in the Kurukshetra war against the Kauravas, Yudhishthira's court priests prevail upon him to perform the great Ashvamedha Yajna, the lighting and nourishing of the sacred fire with oblations of clarified butter in the presence of all the great kings and queens and sages of the land, the resultant aura of multicoloured flames proclaiming the many-hued blessings of the gods for the victorious yajna-celebrant's life and mission in the world.

'Correctly pronounced mantras and the offering of gifts to all guests are a prerequisite for the yajna, as is the letting loose of a horse with an accompanying army. If the yajna is correctly performed, the horse returns unchallenged to the site of the yajna after a year, establishing the supremacy of the yajna-celebrant.

'Yudhishthira's Ashvamedha Yajna is in progress, with his brothers, their common spouse Draupadi, baby grandson Parikshita and Uttara, his widowed mother, sitting close to the yajna fire; and in circles around it, great sovereigns and sages of the land, including the divine Krishna.

'Suddenly, and ominously, a half-golden mongoose enters the marble-floored yajna site, and addresses Yudhishthira in a mocking tone of voice:

Yudhishthira, I am not impressed by your yajna. I thought by rolling on the marble floor of its site, I would become completely golden and liberated from the desire to kill my eternal enemy, the snake. But this has not happened. Listen to my story if you want to know what is lacking in your yajna.

Before the great war which you won, there lived in Kurukshetra a poor brahmana family: father, mother, son and daughter-in-law.

Famine stalked the land. Farmers died of starvation, many committed suicide. The grains in the land were scattered, few and hard to find.

The brahmana family living close to death would collect some grain each day, their only food.

I lived outside their hut and in their generosity they would offer me some of those precious grain to eat.

One day a hungry Chandala visited the family just as they were sitting down to their single meal of the day.

Free of caste prejudice, the father invited the outcaste to share their meal. He offered the guest his portion of the grain, which the Chandala devoured in a moment; however, the meagre offering did not appease his hunger.

The mother, and then the son, offered their share of the grain to the Chandala who ate them but was, of course, still hungry, and looked towards the daughter-in-law, who was pregnant.

The daughter-in-law was about to offer her share of the grain to the Chandala when all three, her husband, father-in-law and mother-in-law, protested.

They reminded the young woman that she was, as predicted by astrologers, carrying their male descendant, and that it was important for her to remain alive, so that she could give birth to a living son and continue the family line.

Yudhishthira, now listen to what this remarkable woman had to say. I was sitting at the door of the hut and witnessed the entire scene.

Addressing her family most respectfully, she said: 'Dear father, mother, husband. First of all, I would like to know why you think the astrologers you have consulted are right in their prediction that I am carrying a son, and not a daughter. Moreover, I think you are wrong in assuming that girls don't continue the family line. Finally, if it is meritorious for all three of you to die rather than fail to appease a guest's hunger, it must be meritorious for me and my unborn baby to make a similar sacrifice.'

And the daughter-in-law also gave her share of the grain to the Chandala, who ate them and was no longer hungry.

The Chandala was Dharma in disguise and had come to test whether or not even a generous and pious family, such as the poor brahmana family, was liberated from prejudice against the girl-child.

Greatly pleased, he revealed his true form, summoned a heavenly chariot and offered to carry the free-spirited daughter-in-law to heaven. She pleaded that the rest of the family should be allowed to accompany her, and so they did.

I was also asked to accompany them, but I preferred to roll on the holy ground where the family, especially the daughter-in-law, had lived, and became half-golden. Had the father, mother and son not been prejudiced in favour of a male-child to continue their line, I would have become completely golden.

Then, many years later, I heard that you were performing the great Ashvamedha Yajna in celebration of your victory in the Kurukshetra war, and I thought I would visit you and become completely golden.

I have not. I am not impressed by your yajna.

I can see that only Uttara and her baby son Parikshita among you are completely golden, completely devoid of dualistic prejudice.

I believe this is because, in order to revive the wounded Parikshita in Uttara's womb, Krishna had assumed the form of a butterfly and entered Uttara's womb with the resources of nature, herbs and grass, and had stitched the torn foetus back to life. Bringing to the 'conception' of a human being dimensions of non-anthropocentric reality, including the dimension of nothingness represented by the nearly dead Parikshita and Uttara.

If Uttara and Parikshita accept me as their friend, I might think better of your yajna, Yudhishthira!

The mongoose walked to where golden Uttara was seated, with her golden son in her lap. Parikshita gurgled with joy at the sight of the half-golden mongoose and Uttara invited him to her seat. Parikshita and the mongoose played with each other. Slowly, the mongoose became completely golden, liberated from his sense of the snake as being 'not-self', implacable enemy.

Yudhishthira, you never sought Draupadi's forgiveness for letting Dushasana disrobe her in Dhritarashtra's court. This is why your yajna was imperfect. But with the blessings of the remarkable daughter-in-law of the brahmana family whose story I have told you, and the acceptance of a despised mongoose by Arjuna's daughter-in-law, Uttara, and his grandson, Parikshita, your yajna's imperfection will be forgiven by your father, Dharma, whose darshana as a Chandala I had the privilege to have.

'That is how the Ashvamedha Yajna was consummated,' concluded Babu.

The informal meeting ended with Debbie thanking Babu and exchanging addresses with him.

It was 1 p.m.

Ravi had lunch at the Tassajara Bakery nearby, spent hours walking the streets of San Francisco, and killed time by watching two bad movies at a theatre on Geary.

He walked into 'The Pub' at 8 p.m.

His favourite rheumatism-friendly seat was occupied. Anna smiled consolingly at Ravi and played 'What a wonderful world!' on the jukebox to cheer him up. Ravi sat on a bar-stool near the pub phone and when Anna brought him his pint, he explained to her that he was expecting an important phone call around 9 p.m.

'No problem, I'll take the call and give you the receiver, and you don't have to be too brief,' she said, simultaneously encouragingly and restrainingly, and disappeared for a while.

At five minutes to nine, Anna took a moment off from work and sat down on the vacant stool next to Ravi's, so as to be able to receive his call and hand it over to him, something Ravi was quick to perceive. But she also had a query about the Ramana story he had told her the previous evening.

'Ravi, what if there is no sun at all? I remember my grandfather, an Auschwitz survivor, telling me that he saw a Rabbi running up and down the yard of the concentration camp, where hundreds of Jews and others were being gassed to death day after day, shouting at the top of his voice: "There is no God! There is no God!" He was shot instantly. Where was the sun in Auschwitz, Ravi?'

Ravi closed his eyes, chanted 'Aum Sri Ramanaya Namah', and found himself telling Anna that the sun was the Rabbi himself and all the victims, who weakened the self-esteem of the evil of racist hatred by their unresisting submission to it. Even the shadow of Nazism, which darkened the earth for years, couldn't have existed without the sun of truth. The shadow would have been put in its place if the powers that be were sun-turned. They were not. British imperialism, which was nothing but institutionalised racism, was not willing to promise independence to India even after the war. The statue of King George V in New Delhi had its back to the sun!'

Anna was about to say something like: 'Bless you, Ravi, but I can still hear that Rabbi's scream!' when she heard the telephone ring. It was 9 p.m.

'Who is on the line? Yes, this is "The Pub". You are Ananya and whom do you want to speak with? Babu? There is no one by that name here, I am afraid,' said Anna.

'That's another name of mine, Anna!' Ravi shouted, and snatched the receiver from her hands. She let him do so, but not without saying, 'You orientals and your many names and gods!'

And the following decisive conversation occurred:

Ravi: 'Is that Muniya? Did you get my message? I mean my telephone message, yes, not the cry: "Where are you Muniya? Where are you my baby girl?" which has been issuing forth from my heart for years now, which, too, I hope you have sometimes heard deep down in your heart.'

Muniya: 'Yes, I got your message, Babu. And I hope you too have sometimes heard, deep down in your heart, the question which Baba and Ayi and I have so often asked all these years: "Why doesn't Babu come to see us any more? Why doesn't he realise that an occasional telephone call from Kolkata, Delhi, Pondicherry, on Sabarmati is no substitute for a meeting?"'

Ravi: 'I plead guilty Muniya, forgive me. But can you fly back home with me? In London we will be the guests of a Gujarati family who have sponsored a lecture, on 'Hinduism and Violence', which they want me to deliver at the Bharatiya Vidya Bhavan, the Indian culture centre.'

Muniya: 'I'll see you at the San Francisco Airport in time for our flight on September 11, Babu. Your travel agent friend has made all arrangements. But how will we recognise each other?'

Babu: 'By your smile, widening eyes and sidewardly moving mouth, and by the grace of Ramana Maharshi, Muniya. Aum, Ayi, Baba, Babu, Chanti, Chanti, Chanti. Are you with me Muniya? Why are you crying?'

Muniya: 'I'll be with you soon, Babu. Enjoy your drink, Bye!'

Babu called Arun late at night and gave him the good news that he and Muniya would be home soon.

Airborne

Ravi was irritated, but not surprised by the physicality which marred the security scrutiny to which all passengers were subjected to on the anniversary of 9/11 at the San Francisco airport. He was troubled by the thought that Muniya, too, would receive a similar security massage, albeit by female hands.

Wheeling his bags to the Air India economy class counter, Ravi waited in the queue, letting others go ahead, because he had not spotted Muniya yet. He wanted adjacent seats for himself and Muniya, not only because this would facilitate conversation and the delicate inquiry which Arun had urged him to make about her state of mind. Sitting 'shoulder to shoulder' with her would also symbolise for him a camaraderie with her, regardless of the enormous age difference between them.

Born in 1944 like Arun, Ravi was fifty-eight years old, and Muniya, born in 1980, was twenty-two. Ravi had last seen her in 1987, when she was seven years old and was being sent off to Sanawar, a school in the Himalayan foothills. A bright tall brown child with a wide forehead and strong chin and an economical style of speaking, comforting a crying Archana: 'You worry too much Ayi, look after Abhinava and yourself and Baba, I'll be well.'

And turning on her illumined smile at Babu when he said, 'Muniya, do well!' she had reciprocated that expectation with identical words. 'Do well, Babu!' she had said.

How would the alchemy of time have sculpted that child into a twenty-two-year-old graduate student of Art and Religion?

There was a sprinkling of young Indian women among the passengers queuing up at the Air India check-in counter, some of whom looked like students and twenty-two-ish, but Ravi was being like the upanishadic rishi who said, 'Neti, Neti, not this, not this ....' to all that failed to image Atman, self, one in all.

'No, that is not Muniya, she is insufficiently weighed-down by world-suffering ...,' and, 'No not even she, that would-be film-star girl, she is insufficiently spontaneously joyous.' Ravi would not take somebody else for Muniya, even if he were to fail to identify her, such was his faith in the self-revelatory power of the form which had imprinted itself on his mind indelibly when he first set eyes on Muniya.

It was September 1984. Ravi, who had spent years in Tiruvannamalai studying the life and thought of Sri Ramana Maharshi, and meditated on him with a growing sense of the sage's presence in his consciousness, had written to his college friend Arun Kulkarni in Pune and asked if he could spend some time with him and his family, and had been warmly invited to do so.

Ravi realised that staying with Arun and Archana and their daughter, Ananya, who would then be four years old, and her two-year-old baby brother Abhinava, was just what Ramana had ordered as a cure for his deepening depression at the thought of the criminal gulf between Advaita's celebration of selfhood and Indian society's refusal to honour selfhood in the girl-child throughout all stages of her life.

Arun had received Ravi at Pune and driven him in his old Ford to his traditional Shaniwarpeth home in the old city, and as Ravi climbed the few steps to the veranda where Archana and Ananya and

Abhinava (in the arms of housemaid Kalpana) were waiting to receive him, Ananya had stepped forward and allowed Ravi to take her into his arms.

'Ananya, I have decided to call you "Muniya", a common name for girls in eastern Uttar Pradesh, a name also of the Divine Mother conceived as a playful bird, a name which has embedded in it the idea of a 'muni', the silent sage, who, like you, doesn't speak much or not at all, but understands the deepest secrets of the human heart.'

Ravi had hardly concluded this philosophical introduction of himself and his understanding of Ananya when the little girl pulled out the fountain pen from his khadi jacket pocket and, to everybody's surprise, called him 'Babu!' a name by which older men are commonly addressed in eastern Uttar Pradesh.

And Muniya had looked Babu straight in the eye, as though they had known each other in many lives, and smiled at him with a swift widening of her eyes and a sideward movement of her closed mouth. (Didn't Minakshi, in the great mural in the Madurai Temple depicting her marriage to Shiva, smile like that?)

That initiating face was timeless and Babu would not forget it till his dying day.

Ravi must have closed his eyes during this lapse into memory and meditation.

That's when he heard the voice he had heard and spoken to on the phone a few days earlier. He knew Muniya had arrived but didn't want to open his eyes immediately and spoil the magic of the moment.

Wordlessly, a hand pulled out the fountain pen from his woollen khadi jacket, and he heard liberating laughter and opened his eyes to find Muniya looking him straight in the eye, with a 'sudden smile of widening eyes and a sideward movement of her closed mouth'.

'Babu, I presume!' said the tall girl in denims. Wide forehead, strong chin, evolved, oval, Modigliani face, a single diamond on her nose, lush black hair coiled into a cobra pigtail, long strong limbs, graduate tiredness, sadness, defiance, openness, light.

'Muniya, meri pyari Muniya, I thought you wouldn't come, I have been waiting for years for you to manifest again in my life!'

Last announcements were being made and obliging Air India staff found adjacent seats for them.

A journey which in this life began in 1984 and had been interrupted by circumstances had resumed.

Babu had heard that the 'lighthouse' radiance of the single diamond which adorned the nose of Kanyakumari's statue in her sea-facing temple at Cape Comorin had led many a storm-tossed ship to land safely on Indian shores.

Wasn't the light of Muniya's smile, which was merely reflected by the diamond on her nose, leading him home?

Remembrance

We have been born many times, Arjuna
I remember all my births, you do not
(BHAGAVADGITA, 4.5)

Beginnings

Arun Kulkarni and Ravi Srivastava went to study at Delhi University in the same year, 1961. Arun made the transition from Doon School, and Ravi from a government school in Allahabad.

Both had won National Entrance Scholarships. Arun took admission in St Stephen's College to study History, and Ravi was denied admission to St Stephen's but happy to be admitted to Hindu College to study philosophy for the BA (Honours) degree.

Scholarship conditions required them to live in their college hostels across the road. St Stephen's shunned the word 'hostel' and chose to describe its residential quarters as 'Residence', somewhat 'tautologically', as the would-be-philosopher Ravi was to point out to a sporting Arun.

It was during the entrance scholarship examinations that the two young men had first met. But it was on the cricket field, in 1961, in a fiercely contested match between Stephen's and Hindu that the two really discovered each other, Arun's bludgeoning batsmanship first flaying and then succumbing to Ravi's leg-break-googly bowling. The youngsters had made a mark as promising cricketers while still at school.

It did not take long for Arun and Ravi to transcend the old rivalry of their colleges and become friends.

Arun went to the extent of inviting Ravi to join St Stephen's cricketers at net practice one winter afternoon, with the permission of his college philosophy teacher and cricket guru, the legendary Bose Saheb, Sudhir Kumar Bose, who even offered Ravi some advice about flight and length and line, which are always difficult to harmonise. Being a good cricketer evidently compensated for being on the wrong side of the road.

It was already dark when, after 'nets', Bose Saheb, Arun and Ravi walked together from the St Stephen's cricket ground to the Kashmiri Gate bus stop. Bose Saheb would take a bus to his haveli in Daryaganj, and the two boys the same bus to their colleges in time for dinner.

The moon was in place in the darkening sky and Ravi, keen to initiate a conversation with Bose Saheb, ventured to show-off the scientific general knowledge he had gathered from his father. His father had been a professor of chemistry at the Allahabad University, until a fatal heart attack a few years earlier.

'Bose Saheb,' Ravi declared, 'We are inclined, especially in our country, to think of the moon not only as an awakener of romantic feelings in young hearts, a maker of waves in consciousness, but as itself possibly a sphere of snow and lakes and rivers. But science has proved beyond a shadow of doubt that the moon is hard, hard, rock!'

When this impassioned 'news' announcement elicited no response from the philosopher, Ravi repeated it at a slow speed for better comprehension.

And there was a response then.

Between puffs of smoke which emanated from Bose Saheb's nostrils (he was believed by his detractors to have been born not with a silver spoon but a cigarette in his mouth), the great man said what Ravi would remember for the rest of his life as his first initiation into independent thought:

'Young man, I wouldn't be so sure, I wouldn't be so sure!'

Years later, Ravi would grasp the deeper meaning of those words, the insight that there was no 'sheer otherness', of which the idea of 'hard, hard, rock' was a powerful symbol.

'I wouldn't be so sure, I wouldn't be so sure!' was to become for Ravi the first response of advaitin caution whenever the supposed 'otherness' of anything, as distinguished from its distinctiveness, was affirmed, be it another person, culture, race, religion, or even divinity.

But that night, in Arun's room, Ravi and Arun bemoaned the paralysing effect of established thought, ancient or modern, on the human mind. Arun laughed at Ravi's googly being hit for a six by Bose Saheb.

In 1962 when China invaded India, and privileged students of Delhi University thought it sufficient to merely discuss the leading articles on the subject in the daily newspapers, Arun and Ravi strongly felt that they should defy conventional middle-class wisdom and join the Indian Army and defend their country, sacrificing their academic careers.

They sought Bose Saheb's approval of their plans. His answer defied the received wisdom of patriotism.

'Arun, Ravi, you will be better patriots after completing your studies and improving your batting and bowling and, if I may add, your fielding.'

After graduation Arun joined the Indian Air Force, became a squadron leader, and saw action in the 1971 war against Pakistan and received a high gallantry award.

However, because Indira Gandhi didn't press home the advantage of India's victory in the 1971 war, Arun resigned from the Air Force and settled down to a life of premature retirement in his ancestral home in Pune. (His father, Shrikant Kulkarni, had been an officer in the Indian Navy and had taken part in the naval mutiny in the Mumbai docks in 1946. He, too, had quit the armed forces because he felt that independent India had not treated the mutineers with justice. Dejected, alcoholism caused his premature death in the same year that Ravi's father had died. This coincidence strengthened the bond of friendship between Arun and Ravi.)

After graduation, Ravi won a scholarship to study philosophy at the University of Aberdeen in Scotland. He stayed on to receive a doctorate degree. But he was deeply dissatisfied with the absence of any serious engagement with the reality of selfhood in contemporary British-American philosophy and returned to India to study Indian traditions of inquiry into selfhood, especially Advaita Vedanta.

The mid-1970s found Ravi deeply absorbed in the life and thought of Sri Ramana Maharshi, the sage who attained self-realisation in 1896 at the age of sixteen and taught the truth of Atman, self, in the sacred town of Tiruvannamalai in Tamil Nadu, until his death in 1950.

Ravi made a small hotel room in Tiruvannamalai his home.

His mother had died just before he left India for Britain in 1964, and Ravi couldn't bear the thought of living in Allahabad without her.

An only child, he thought of Sri Ramana as his mother and father, 'Amma-Appa' in Tamil, a language in which he had gained a modest proficiency. He lived austerely but contentedly on incomes from tuitions in the town of Tiruvannamalai.

And Ravi knew that in Arun he had more than a brother, a kindred spirit who wanted India to rediscover the inclusive wisdom of Hinduism to nourish its hard-won independence and serve the world. They wrote to each other from time to time. Arun worked as a consultant for a number of airlines and led a simple life, and was generous to a fault.

Ravi was especially delighted when Arun informed him that he had married Archana, a vivacious young woman who was devoted to the service of the oppressed sections of Hindu society.

In 1980 a girl was born to Arun and Archana, after Arun's mother, Lakshmibai, made a pilgrimage to Alandi to offer a petitionary prayer to Jnaneshvara Maharaj for a grandchild.

The girl was named 'Ananya' (meaning 'no other, self') at Ravi's suggestion.

And two years later, in 1982, Arun and Archana were blessed with a baby boy, whom his grandmother called 'Abhinava'.

Ananya was greatly devoted to her grandmother, and she to her.

But Lakshmibai's deepest regret before she died a year later, in 1983, was that her granddaughter, Ananya, hadn't spoken a complete sentence yet, although she was three years old.

Arun and Archana took Ananya to Mumbai to consult speech specialists who found there wasn't anything wrong with the little girl at all.

But Ananya remained stubbornly speechless, refusing invitations to speak with her defiant little chin and tightly pursed lips.

Ravi wrote to Arun and Archana and expressed his desire to spend some time with them.

Arun asked Ravi to take the next convenient train to Pune.

Thanksgiving

Ravi was overwhelmed by Arun and Archana's unhesitating invitation to him to spend some time with them in Pune.

He had spent several years in Tiruvannamalai, not exchanging his small hotel room for better accommodation because its only window (which Ravi never shut) offered a glorious view of Arunachala: the massive, bouldery, shouldery, many-peaked hill, apparently inert, but in reality none other than vibrant self-awareness: Shiva himself had summoned to its caves (consciousness has its hiding places for its fugitive devotees) young Ramana from Madurai where the athletic lad had extracted from the fear of death the fearlessness of moksha, self-realisation.

Ravi stood at the window of his room with closed eyes and folded hands, and poured out his heart to his 'Appa'.

Appa! Ramana! You saved my life when I thought I would never be able to see my way out of the dead-end of the now dominant philosophical dogma that consciousness is always only conscious of something other than itself, never of itself, there being no 'self' at all.

This dogma makes consciousness a slave of all objects, things, processes, thoughts, theories, whatever, of which, and never of itself, consciousness is supposed to be conscious of.

A Street in Tiruvannamalai

The ensnaring consumerism of our times, which threatens to become a global temptation, is surely rooted in this harlot view of consciousness, is it not, Appa?

In your hauntingly beautiful *A Marital Garland of Letters*, you implore your lover, Arunachala, to make you one with him, lest your 'harlot mind' should walk the streets forever.

Appa! In that poetical thought you do not merely, and matchlessly, exemplify the erotic symbolism of mystical union, and indicate the hospitableness of brahmacharya to sexuality in the sport of self-realisation.

Appa! In your love letter to Arunachala, you say that harlotry will be your fate if he doesn't 'embrace' you, make you one with him, after abducting you from your home.

Appa! You lured me to your feet when I returned from Britain deeply disenchanted with modern western philosophy's neglect of the reality of selfhood.

I felt something of your embrace, some escape from street-walking, when it dawned on me one day some years ago, right here in this hotel-cave of yours that undeniable self-awareness ('I') would cease to be self-awareness if it were ever aware of 'not-self', objects, not itself.

But wasn't I surrounded by not-self? That bonded child-servant in the hotel down the road with a scar on his face and revenge in his eyes, clearing and cleaning eating tables like an angry world-dissolving Shiva, was he not not-self?

And all the violence and chaos of everyday life in all its dimensions, small, medium, and large-scale, isn't that not-self, Appa!

You took pity upon me and brought to me the liberating thought that what we encountered was only apparent not-self, not real not-self, and that even our own personhood, our "body", was also only apparent self, not real self.

Neither real self nor real not-self, our bodies and all else, including nothingness, could only be self-images of selfhood, self-awareness.

Self-awareness would then not be 'not-self-awareness', but, without ceasing to be self-awareness, awareness of the limitless diversity of its own self-imaging, gross or subtle, luminous or dark.

And this would be your fuller embrace, demanding of us that we bring to that scarred child-servant-boy the freedom and joy of a decent life.

Appa! In your love letter to Arunachala you also ask him what 'the world' would say if he did not make you one with him in the full depth and width of his self-awareness.

I have taken this to mean that we are not fully self-aware until we are able to see the whole 'world' as an image, or an image-in-making, of ourselves.

With this gift of understanding, Appa, you saved my life, because without it, Advaita often seemed to me like absent-mindedness, even as modern western philosophy looks like hypocrisy, and life as a philosopher or as consciousness didn't seem worth living to me.

After unburdening himself of this piece of philosophical-spiritual autobiography, and offering it to Ramana-Arunachala for correction or rejection, Ravi lay down on his floor bed in shavasana, the 'death-asana', because his despair was not yet at an end.

Ravi was troubled by the fate of children in his country, and the thought of the stunted life of the scarred servant-boy in the hotel where he often ate kept him awake with an unappeasable conscience.

'Appa!' his heart cried again, 'Bless me, a Kayastha devotee of yours from Uttar Pradesh, with insight into something in the world of appearance which was a perfect portrait of Atman, absolute certainty, like your face!

'I don't want to jump into unenlightened activism, or remain asleep in insensitive quietism, show me a way out, or take me away!'

Ravi must have fallen asleep at that point of his demanding supplication of Ramana.

But later in the afternoon when, awake and washed, he walked down to the hotel served by the scarred servant-boy, among other slaves, and sat down to have his afternoon filter coffee and idlis, the same child smiled at him, and then, in his place, Ravi saw a girl-servant!

The girl looked at him with a sudden widening of eyes and a sideward movement of her closed mouth and disappeared. Was this hallucination or revelation?

Ravi sipped his coffee, slowly and with a special effort of concentrated thinking, dedicating the exercise to Minakshi of Madurai and her child Ramana.

Light filtered through to his troubled heart. He saw in a flash that what we are absolutely certain of in life was not that we were born (we don't remember our birth), nor that we will die (we can't conceive of our non-existence), but that we are or have been children.

The condition of childhood, therefore, was the perfect picture of Atman, self, about which alone we are absolutely certain in the interiority of our being.

And also (Ravi saw the thought that was now forming in his mind as the gift of the 'hallucinated' boy-and-girl figure in the hotel), our certainty regarding our childhood was unavoidably accompanied by the memory of a feminine form, our mother, or some other woman (a grown girl-child), who held us close to herself and who, however briefly, was undetachable in our consciousness from ourselves: in the way in which, in self-awareness, self is undetachable from itself.

Ravi realised that the tormented servant-boy had self-effacingly manifested as a feminine form and then disappeared to unveil in his heart this unexcellable portrait of Atman, the form of a girl-child, with the realisation that when we harm the girl-child at any stage of her life, embryonic or geriatric, we harm ourselves deeply. And as he walked to the telegraph office to wire details of his arrival in Pune to Arun and Archana, he sensed that Ramana had made him do homework for some important task he was meant to do in Pune.

And then he was literally waylaid by an etymological thought that stopped him in his tracks and made him feel happier than he had ever been in his life.

The word 'Muniya' flew into his mind like the Divine Bird addressed by that same name in eastern Uttar Pradesh, a form of Parvati herself. Embedded in the word 'Muniya' was the idea of the 'muni', the silent sage.

Ananya was 'Muniya', a silent sage! All she needed was to be reminded of her reality, and she might break her apparent vow of silence and flow into speech! Walking briskly to the telegraph office, Ravi wired his travel details to Arun, with 'blessings' to Muniya and Abhinava.

Back in his room, Ravi sat at his writing table, facing Ramana's watchful photograph, and submitted his by now deeply entrenched conviction that the girl-child was the most perfect picture of Atman, to the following scribbling test:

Yes, environing nothingness is a powerful image of Atman's 'not-thingness', self's not being something as opposed to something else.

So is pervasive materiality in its exceptionless lawfulness a self-image of what is, self, which never ceases to be aware of itself.

And also non-human life in its massive self-restraint, its renunciation of violence beyond the necessities of survival.

And ethical and ecological sensitivity, insufficiently exemplified though they are in human life, bear witness to our frequent overcoming of dualist identity and unfold the unity of the habitat of self, rich with the diversity of its self-images.

What about reproductivity and sexuality, which do not characterise childhood, except when childhood is abused? Do they not image self?

No, if reproductivity is an insecure or expansionist multiplication of one's own kind, it cannot, except as caricature, image the autonomy, self-sufficiency, svaraj, of selfhood.

Sri Ramana Maharshi as a youth and his mother Alagammal

Nor can sexuality image the joy of self-realisation if it is not consenual and playful and a sadhana of dissolving the salt-doll of ego in the ocean of love.

And selfhood is of course gloriously imaged in joyous, uncoerced, non-misogynist, brahmacharya.

'And yet,' Ravi wrote, 'As distinguished from self-images of self that are intelligible only to reflection, the condition of childhood with its companion femininity (brought together in the singular image of the girl-child) is, as an evocation of the reality of Atman, unparalleledly luminous.'

Standing at the open window of his room, Ravi folded his hands and closed his eyes in grateful obeisance to Arunachala-Ramana.

Miracle In Pune

Archana emptied a room upstairs which had served as a storeroom for old pieces of furniture and Kalpana, the housemaid, washed and swept it. Aware of his rheumatism, Archana laid a hard cotton mattress on the floor for Babu to sleep on. A mosquito net with long strings attached to its corners was placed on the side of the floor-bed. Babu was a practised mosquito-net user and assured Archana that he would have no difficulty in setting up the protective tent at night with the strings attached to the iron grill of the window which looked out on to the lush mango tree in the courtyard outside.

A hard wooden chair and a large table in the room were to serve Babu's writing and studying needs during his stay in the Kulkarni home.

With Archana's permission (granted with a smile which said, 'You don't have to seek permission for this, this is not only your room but also your home') Babu removed a framed painting of an ancestor of the Kulkarni's, a Peshwa hero, from the wall, placed it inside the built-in wall-shelf in the room which was filled with works of detective fiction, and hung in its place a framed photograph of Ramana Maharshi he had brought with him from Tiruvannamalai as a gift for the Kulkarni home.

'Appa!' he prayed, looking at the radiant photograph, 'Help me persuade Muniya to speak, and may I be helped by her to talk less!'

Catching up on what felt like years of insufficient sleep to him, Babu slept for a full three hours after a sumptuous lunch. Archana sent Ananya upstairs to call Babu down for tea, which she did by sitting down on the floor near Babu's head and pressing it gently with her little palms.

Babu's eyes opened and he realised that Muniya had now initiated him by 'touch', after doing so by 'look' in the veranda in the morning, and before he could say 'Aum Sri Ramanaya Namah', the little girl ran downstairs, giggling all the way, her task accomplished.

Yes, Babu understood that Muniya had successfully communicated Archana's summons to tea, but he recalled Sri Ramakrishna's teaching that initiation is by look, touch and thought. How could he be sure that Muniya would think of him in the way a guru thinks of a shishya, as self, Atman, thereby initiating him into the sadhana of self-realisation? Is Muniya a guru then?

Babu had no doubt at all now that Ramana Maharshi had brought him into contact with Muniya to understand all these matters deeply. If only she would speak! Her calling him 'Babu' was a challenge to him to try and make her want to speak.

'Aum' encompasses all speech, represented by the escalating 'A' sound, and silence, represented by the fading 'M' sound. Babu prayed to Ramana in his heart for strength to persuade little Muniya to chant 'Aum', and walked down the staircase chanting "Aum", Appa, Muniya!' a mantra he felt would stay with him forever.

Birthday

Babu had arrived in Pune towards the end of September, only a few days before Muniya's birthday on 2nd October, which she shared with Mahatma Gandhi, and four days after which, on 6th October, was Vijayadashami.

On the night of 1st October sitting at his writing table facing the photograph of Ramana Maharshi, Babu opened the fat sketchbook he had bought earlier in the day from a stationary store at the Deccan Gymkhana as a birthday gift for Muniya and inscribed the sacred sign 'Aum' on the first sheet, not on the top but right in the middle of it, and not 'From Babu, with love and gratitude'.

'Aum' is itself the giver of the gift, the gift, and the receiver of the gift, he said to himself, in the refrain of the first mantra of the Mandukya Upanishad which declares that whatever is in the past, the present, and the future, and even beyond time, is but 'Aum'.

On 2nd October, he would tell Muniya all he understood of 'A', the first letter of the word 'Aum', to mean. On 3rd, 4th, and 5th October, he would, successively, make a presentation to her of his understanding of the letter-parts 'U' and 'M' and the letterless silence of the fourth, all-encompassing dimension of the syllable which is not merely a symbol, but the very substance, also, of Atman and Brahman, self and purna and shunya.

If his prayers to Ramana, Arunachala, and Minakshi were answered, then on 6th October, that is, on Vijayadashami, the day of the victory of self-realisation over self-obscuration, which is how Babu saw the victory of Durga over Mahishasura, Muniya would utter the mantra 'Aum' and overcome the Mahishasura of her parents' anxiety regarding her speaking capabilities. And bring to Babu's study of Advaita Vedanta and Ramana Maharshi, which had nourished his mind and pacified his anxious heart, the element of joy whose absence he had felt painfully, a sense of the playfulness of self-awareness without which the idea of self-realisation had seemed incomplete to him.

With these thoughts becoming a coherent prayer in his mind, Babu switched off the light in his room and entered his mosquito-proof tent with the aid of a torch and drifted into sleep, sailing silently through the night towards the dawn of Muniya's birthday and his rebirth day.

Babu was awakened in the morning by the sound of little footsteps in his room and he saw Muniya, with tightly pursed lips and chin chiselled with determination, doodling invisible figures on the walls of his tent with her fingers.

His sleepy 'Happy Birthday Muniya!' didn't bring about any change in the child's doodling exercise. At this Babu's thoughts turned to Mahatma Gandhi and his days of silence when he refrained from speaking but often wrote answers to urgent inquiries related to the conduct of satyagraha and the fate of svaraj.

'Pyari Muniya, don't be anxious. I have brought for you, as a birthday gift, a sketchbook, in which you can doodle to your heart's content with the crayons, which come with the sketchbook. You don't have to speak. I'll take today to be your day of silence, like Gandhiji's, who was also born on 2nd October. But will you promise to listen carefully to what I want to talk to you about today?' Babu asked, in a tone both placatory and anxious which melted Muniya's face into a compassionate smile and brought forth from her intuitive heart an encouraging giggle.

And Babu was able to proclaim, without the slightest sense of the unlikelihood of being understood, that he wanted to share with her on her birthday the significance of the first letter of the word 'Aum', the letter 'A', which embodied the significance of wakefulness, of all history and happening, great and small.

Muniya executed her doodling (invisible to ordinary eyes) inscription with both her left and right forefingers on all four sides of the mosquito net, and then ran quickly downstairs, but with a frown, in response to Archana's summons to a birthday oil-bath.

For Babu, Muniya had inscribed nothing less than the fourfold portrayal of reality in the Mandukya Upanishad: as the waking, dream, and sleep states of consciousness in interrelationship, located within the immediacy of self-awareness as pictures of ourselves.

And in her use of both the right and the left forefingers, Babu asked himself, was she not being like Gandhi, her birthday-mate, who wrote the classic work Hind Svaraj with his right hand and, when his right hand was tired, continued to write with his left, refusing to regard the left hand as an unworthy instrument in the performance of sacred tasks?

Washed and bathed, Babu joined the others around the dining table, taking his seat opposite Muniya who enjoyed the birthday privilege of sitting at the head of the table, with Arun and Archana and Abhinava (in a special baby chair) around her.

Muniya was wearing a billowy ankle-length gold-bordered white salwar which looked like a traditional Maharashtrian sari and a short high-necked (gold-bordered like the salwar) kurta which had mirror-work all over it. Archana had designed and stitched this birthday suit for Muniya out of a khadi 'thaan', which Babu had brought for her from Tiruvannamalai.

There was to this striking costume a suggestion of Gandhi's proletarian dhoti and also something of the martial spirit of Lakshmibai, the Rani of Jhansi, but the gold and the mirrors invested the suit with a striking femininity and Muniya glowed like Minakshi of Madurai must have done as a child, the divine princess of the Pandyan Empire.

At Arun's suggestion, Babu chanted 'Aum Sri Ramanaya Namah', his mantra of obeisance to Ramana Maharshi, and added in Hindi the prayer – 'Tu jiye hazaaron saal, har saal ke din hon pachaas hazaar' – wishing Muniya a long life.

Uppama (a concession to Babu's long residence in South India) and puran poli were the special features of the birthday feast which Muniya tucked into with great delight, to Archana's amazement, for without her cajoling coerciveness Muniya rarely finished a meal.

After breakfast, Arun drove off to the Pune Club to meet some old air force batch-mates who were in town, leaving Abhinava with Kalpana and Muniya with Babu. Archana took a three-wheeler to join fellow social workers at the Indian Institute of Education in Kothrud where a celebration of Gandhi Jayanti and a discussion of his thoughts on rural reconstruction had been planned.

Sprawled on the living room floor near the Ganapati bronze, a family heirloom, Muniya opened her sketchbook and held crayons in both hands, all set like the elephant deity, Babu thought, to inscribe anything that Babu might have to tell her about 'Aum' which would measure up to standards set by Vyasa.

Terrified of failure, Babu prayed to Ramana for strength.

Reclining on the jhoola at the other end of the living room, opposite the Ganapati image, Babu stared at the ceiling, and began stutteringly to expostulate what the Mandukya Upanishad says about 'Aum'.

Sensing Babu's diffidence, Muniya walked up to the jhoola and gave it a tug and returned to her writing site.

The gentle swaying of the jhoola made Babu start all over again, more playfully, and he found himself making the following remarks as though self-knowledge lodged in Muniya's heart was speaking through him. As though 'Aum' were Muniya and she was talking about herself. In her own yet-to-be-heard voice!

> I am all things, past, present and future. Because I do not remember being born, if I was born at all. And I will not be aware of dying, if I were to die at all. I cannot only be this body, this person, this child, this mute cause of anxiety to her parents.
>
> I must be all forms and also that which is without form, I am speech and silence. Being and nothingness. Purna and shunya.
>
> I am wakefulness, work, signalled by the letter-sound 'A'. But not only activism. I am also contemplativeness.
>
> I am Gandhi's frenzied 'Quit India' call in 1942, which destroyed the prestige of racism.
>
> I am also his intriguing patience and apparent quiescence in 1947, which preserved Indian independence and the honour of India's spiritual traditions.
>
> I am Krishna's refusal to let Arjuna run away from a just war. I am also Krishna's readiness to do nothing but wait for a hungry hunter, who took him to be a deer, to kill him. I, Krishna, actually became a deer, so as to nourish life.
>
> I am ethically and ecologically sensitive wakefulness. Yes, I am 'A', the letter-sound of initiation.

Babu was in a trance of non-dualist identification with Muniya's heart of illumination and his readings aloud of that text of self-knowledge were now unstoppable.

Muniya's Ganapati writings in crayon kept pace with Babu's speech for a long time, but the little girl got tired eventually and, without disturbing Babu's divinations, she tiptoed out of the jhoola room to play with Abhinava. But not before running upstairs to Babu's room and placing her sketchbook on his writing desk for him to read her twelve sheets of Jackson Pollockian correlates of the twelve mantras of the Mandukya Upanishad in the quiet hours of the night when Pune, and Muniya, slept.

Arun and Archana returned from their engagements around noon and found Babu lying on the jhoola, eyes closed, and talking to himself. Not wanting to disturb what they took to be a compositional exercise of his for later conversion into writing, but intrigued by the rhythm of his speech, they sat down near the Ganapati bronze. And this is what they heard Babu say:

I am 'A', yes, as in Ananya, which means no other, self, you!. I am you, and all forms, and formlessness too.'

'I am Buddhism and Vedanta' (Archana was dumbfounded. At the Kothrud meeting there had been a fierce debate between Ambedkarite Buddhists and Gandhian Vedantins). 'The wisdom of un-self-deceiving wakefulness which does not jettison unity because of the challenge of diversity.' (It was Arun's turn to be amazed. At the club he and his erstwhile air force comrades-in-arms had talked, with agitation, about growing Sikh-Hindu differences in the Punjab, and the danger of these differences obscuring the deeply Hindu symbolism of Sikh bhakti and shakti which had brought revolutionary fervour to complacent Hinduism in recent centuries, and a sense of antiquity to Sikhism.)

I am 'U' too, as in 'Uttara', which means 'the awaited one'. The wisdom of dreaming, the awaited capability of seekers of moksha and nirvana to see the world not as illusion but as a theatre or cinema of self-images of purna and shunya, the art-work of illumination, ethical and ecological and existential sensitivity.

And I am also 'M', as in 'Muniya'. The silence of restful sleep and large-hearted renunciation, the peace of patience beyond the greed of competitiveness.

And beyond and behind wakefulness, dreaming and sleep, I am abiding freshness, 'abhinava', unfading self-awareness. I am Ananya and Abhinava too.

I am 'Aum'.

Precisely at this point, Kalpana entered the living room with Abhinava in her arms and a beaming Muniya.

Babu was awakened from his trance. And all watched Muniya hide behind the Ganapati image and intone, with indisputable, sing-song, authority, her birthday declaration:

'Aum. Ayi. Baba. Abhinava. Babu. Aum.'

Arun made telephone calls to friends in Fergusson College and arranged for special net-practice for the college cricket team that evening (he was honorary coach to the team).

Because Mahishasura had been hit for a six by Durga several days ahead of Vijayadashami.

Jnaneshvari

Early in the morning after the awakening of the shakti of speech in Muniya the night before, Babu decided to undertake a pilgrimage of thanksgiving to Alandi, Jnaneshvara Maharaj's samadhi not far from Pune.

Arun, with the entire family (and Kalpana) filling up the old Ford, drove him to the Maharashtra state bus stop.

Babu blew a kiss to Muniya from his window, and although the roar of the unserviced engines of the Pune-Alandi state transport bus prevented him from hearing what she, standing outside and waving both arms sankeertana style, was saying, he could lip-read the 'Aum' Muniya was chanting. And he shouted 'Aum Sri Ramanaya Namah', 'Aum Sri Jnanesvaraya Namah', 'Aum Sri Muniyaya Namah!' as the pilgrim-packed vehicle hit the highway.

Lost in contemplation, Babu's thoughts turned to Sri Krishna and Jnaneshvara Maharaj's extraordinary commentary on the Bhagavadgita, the famed *Jnaneshvari*, which he had read in an English translation that was implausible when it was not inelegant, and hoped that at Alandi a Hindi translation of the masterpiece would be available as he did not read Marathi.

Babu recalled a lunch hosted by a Gujarati family in Delhi years ago where a Gujarati kathavachaka, a storyteller, had held forth on the menu of the great feast during Yudhishthira's Rajasuya Yajna, before the Kurukshetra war.

The storyteller spoke in Hindi, because many guests like Babu did not know Gujarati, but the menu of the ancient feast as described by the storyteller consisted entirely of choice Gujarati dishes – chhunda, dhokla, osaman, puran poli, et al – and while that was appetising, everybody missed the relevance of the culinary discourse to the Mahabharata.

Sensing the discomfiture of his audience, the storyteller suddenly confronted them with a question.

'Dear friends,' he asked, 'Who do you think cleared the litter of leaf-plates left behind by the kings and queens at the Rajasuya feast?'

As nobody knew, the storyteller compassionately revealed that the menial task was performed by none other than Sri Krishna himself.

Babu recalled that when the storyteller delivered this punch line, he had felt that there could be no doubt about the historicity of Sri Krishna, that the performance of the cleaning-up task by God-incarnate Krishna could not have been imagined by a caste-oppressive society: the job must have been done by a real person.

And wasn't Sri Krishna, Arjuna's spiritual father, a charioteer, like Karna's foster father?

Can it be right to demand of modern shudras, as their contemporary leaders do, that they sever all links with caste-transcending Krishna, spiritual father and mother of all?

And do modern caste-prejudiced Hindus have the right to worship Krishna who renounced even the caste of humanity by becoming a deer (Babu was convinced that that is the correct reading of the manner of Krishna's death) to enable a hungry hunter to kill and eat him?

Sri Jnaneshvara Maharaj

'Ramana, make it possible for me some day to explain all this to Muniya!' Babu prayed, and dozed off. Alandi was still a couple of hours away.

Babu's deep sleep of thanksgiving was an anjali, an offering of all images (gross or subtle) to the formless divine, and he was not jolted into wakefulness by the frenzied driving of the state transport bus.

But the divine is both formless and with form, as Sri Ramakrishna had reminded the world more than a century and a half ago, inaugurating a new age of integral spirituality of which India alone could be a trustee: Hinduism, especially, did not ostracise any tradition of worshipping the divine as blasphemous.

This thought must have lain like a seed in the depths of Babu's slumber, waiting to blossom as a dream, and so it did, triggered by the conductor's whistle as he brought the bus to a halt at an unscheduled stop to let some farmers get off near a sugar-cane field through which a dirt track led to their village.

It could have been a darker, yet more luminous, variation of a scene in a film by Satyajit Ray or Ritwik Ghatak, distinctively Bengal school, that now flashed on Babu's screen of somnambulant consciousness, and he became aware of three figures walking slowly through the garden of a large nineteenth century estate of a Kolkata zamindar.

The figure in the middle, like Sri Ramana, had a head of white hair and a short white beard, dream-cinema's trademark, upanishadic, interpolation of ambiguity in the texts of wakefulness, because the form of the figure, including the black Bengali bhadralok jacket and red-bordered dhoti, was unmistakably that of Sri Ramakrishna Paramahamsa.

And jumping nearly a century ahead, the dream footage showed Ramakrishna, Gandhi-like, walking with his arms resting on the shoulders of the other two figures.

One of them was a college boy in cricket whites, whom Babu recognised straightaway as himself in his first year as an undergraduate at Hindu College in Delhi, Thakur's left arm resting across his shoulders.

The other figure was a complete stranger to Babu, a young woman with a broad chin. The graduate student's scholastic maturity and anxiety were visible on her wide forehead and long face, her shoulders providing a resting place for Thakur's right arm. She wore denims and long hair and a diamond on her nose.

Ramakrishna was speaking to the two students in English with a pronounced British accent which Babu thought was like Peter Strawson's, the Oxford philosopher who during a visit to the University of Aberdeen in Scotland, where Babu was a research student, had made a great impression on faculty and students alike. (So much for Ramakrishna's supposed racism, thought Babu's dream-mind).

It was as if this thought had been transmitted to Babu by the denim devotee, because she looked at him with a widening of her eyes and a simultaneous sideward movement of her mouth precisely at the moment the thought occurred to Babu. Muniya? Twenty years from now?

As if to allay all this cinematic anxiety, Ramakrishna pointed out the estate manager's house which stood a hundred yards in front of them, and spoke these magical words:

'Babu and Muniya!' he said, 'That house we see, and this garden, are not real, because they may disappear entirely in a few hundred years as a result of humanity's annihilationist proclivity, unlike reality which is ever-present. And yet they cannot be unreal, because we can see them with our eyes. They are not, like a square circle, an unencounterable impossibility (here Ramakrishna's voice sounded absolutely indistinguishable from Strawson's).

'So the house and the garden, like human life surrounded by nature, are neither real nor unreal, they are more like a cinema-in-the-making. We are trustees, not owners, of our lives and of nature. We must allow Atman, our selfhood and deepest reality of self-awareness, to make adequate self-images out of the malleability of life and time on earth, manifesting ethical and ecological and existential responsibility: portraits of reality, of being and nothingness.

'Life is Lila!' Thakur said emphatically.

Precisely at this point Babu was awakened by the sounds of devotional singing to which some of the pilgrims on the bus had resorted to.

Veering round and round in its own raucous lila, the bus found parking space inside the Alandi bus shed.

'Ramana has blessed me with a vision of Muniya in the future! May I live long enough to witness that vision become reality!' Babu exclaimed as he got off the bus shakingly, resting his arms on the obliging shoulders of two pilgrims, who shouted, 'Hare Krishna!'

The Alandi shrine of Jnaneshvara Maharaj consists of an inner courtyard which has a rectangular stone slab (a flat television screen for a clear vision of self?) marking his Mahasamadhi (at the age of twenty!), and an adjoining room where he had entered to meditate but when, after several hours, the room was opened by devotees, there was no one in the room: the sage had dematerialised, as we would say in our science-fiction-influenced idiom, whereas it would be spiritually more accurate to say that he had adorned the garment of nothingness.

The samadhi slab was a trustee of nothingness. Balanced, on all fours, 'chatushpat', like a four-footed animal, or the fourth varna felled by self-distorting Hindu orthodoxy, as the Mandukya Upanishad would appear to suggest. Atman-Brahman hidden in its oppressed forms.

The Bhagavadgita, on which Jnaneshvara's commentary was regarded by Babu as unsurpassable, is a teaching distinguished by its comprehensiveness, its irreducibility to sectarian one-sidedness. It suddenly seemed appropriate to Babu that the sage should, in order to underscore dramatically the wholeness of the Gita's divine song, manifest the form (or formlessness) of nothingness also, so as not to encourage us to regard the reality of Sri Krishna, Atman, as confined to his dazzling form alone, but as also encompassing nothingness or emptiness.

Perhaps Jnaneshvara's was the earliest attempt to bring Buddhism and Vedanta into harmony with one another and to connect both with Christianity's faith in the empty tomb of Christ, who Babu thought was the first martyr of Advaita.

Babu had always felt that the resurrection of Christ's body was only a metaphor of the ever-presentness of the form of the self-realised sage to the call of devotion, mistakenly construed in Christian theology as the eternally fixed form of imperishability.

But these thoughts had never occurred to Babu before in their wide-ranging togetherness, and he felt certain that they had been imparted to him by the initiating gesture of the young woman of his recent dream on the bus to Alandi: widening of eyes and simultaneous sideward movement of mouth, Muniya-like.

Babu decided to give that form a name appropriate to his pilgrimage to Alandi: he called the girl 'Jnaneshvari', the name Jnaneshvara had given his commentary on the Gita.

Jnaneshvari, divinity of higher knowledge or wisdom, paired with cricket's duality-dissolving playfulness, supporting India's contribution to the rediscovery of integral spirituality in the modern world.

Muniya's 'Aum, Chanti, Chanti, Chanti!' incantation resonated in Babu's ears as he visualised Alandi becoming in the future a major pilgrimage site for a world hungry for inclusive truth.

Babu was in no hurry to catch an early bus back to Pune. The revolutionary, ecumenical, possibilities of understanding the significance of Jnaneshvara's samadhi which were embedded in his upanishadic bus dream, which again was no doubt the fruit of the blessing of little Muniya's 'bon voyage' chanting of 'Aum' at the bus station in Pune, called for a contemplative visit to the chai shack across the road from the shrine.

Babu sat on the long bench outside the shack, sipping piping hot chai from a large metal glass in which, at his request, it had been served to him, and fell into conversation with two men of unspecifiable caste who sat on either side of him, who were also drinking chai served to them more conventionally in clay vessels.

The older man sitting on his left put aside the newspaper he was reading (an act suggestive of a resolve to go beyond received, recorded opinion) and asked Babu (who looked obviously like a pilgrim from another place and not a resident of Alandi) what he thought was the truth about Jnaneshvara's disappearance into thin air, as one stream of tradition would have us believe, adding, that if that were the case, the samadhi structure could have no meaning, because such structures are traditionally built around the deceased bodies of sages in the seated meditational asana.

Before Babu could venture a response to that acute inquiry of (possibly) neo-Buddhist, Dalit, inspiration, the younger man sitting on his right delivered a more straightforwardly suspicious judgement.

'Jnaneshvara's brahmana father had been a sannyasin who had returned to the life of a householder and fathered four children, an alleged spiritual regression regarded as unforgivably sinful by Hindu orthodoxy,' the man stated, factually correctly enough, and he turned around and looked at other customers in the chai shack as if to say, 'Can you deny that?'

No denial was forthcoming, and so the speaker (who now had all patrons of the street restaurant paying close attention to him) went on, heatedly, to spell out his judgement.

'The ceaseless humiliations that were hurled upon them and their children by the ruling caste elite forced Jnaneshvara's parents to drown themselves. And Jnaneshvara and his siblings had to allow themselves to be buried alive, the gruesome ritual passing off as the traditional installation of a samadhi for a sage.'

There was commotion in the chai shack as the speaker had gone beyond recounting facts and appeared to be denigrating saintliness in suggesting that Jnaneshvara and his siblings lacked the courage to challenge the prejudices of oppressive orthodoxy.

Babu got up from 'the bench' (a dissenting member of 'the bench'?) and brought the inflammable situation under control by greeting everybody with a namaskara offered with closed eyes (and an emergency silent chanting of the mantra 'Aum Sri Ramanaya Namah').

'Whatever may have been the cause of Jnaneshvara's parents drowning themselves,' he said, 'And certainly the hard-heartedness of orthodoxy must have played its part in necessitating that act, there can be no doubt that Jnaneshvara, young and truthful like Naciketa before him, would not have been received by Yama without embarrassment. Yama would have granted him the shroud of invisibility, the sacred garment of emptiness, to draw attention in an unforgettable, dramatic way, to the truth that we are not identical with our bodies, whatever be our caste.

'And to draw attention to the equally important truth that it cannot be that we are not our bodies at all, that our bodies are self-images of selfhood, trustees of the light of self-awareness, a samadhi structure had to be built to symbolise precisely this custodianship of the limitless (purna or shunya) by the limited.

'And let me remind you of that comical episode of profound significance, when an angry sadhu seated on a lion (now he shouldn't have usurped Durga's vahana, who is also Jnaneshvari, should he?) approached Jnaneshvara and his siblings who were sitting on a wall, with the intention of at least blaming the children for the supposed sin of their parents in begetting them. Instead of running away from danger, Jnaneshvara caused the wall bearing him and his siblings to move towards the sadhu out of respect for his holiness.

'Dear friends, it is not so difficult to learn to sit on the back of a lion, any circus clown could teach you to do that. But to move walls which separate us from supposed others, now that is indeed difficult but not impossible, as Jnaneshvara showed. And to overcome the barrier which separates being from nothingness, Vedanta from Buddhism, Jnaneshvara embraced emptiness, without ceasing to be self. That, at least, is the mystery and message of the Alandi samadhi of Jnaneshvara Maharaj.'

Thus concluding his dissenting but reconciling intervention, which was greeted by the café audience with reflective silence, Babu decided to board the next bus back to Pune and walked briskly to the bus station which was only a short distance away from the shrine.

There was no time, alas, to look for a Hindi translation of the Jnaneshvari.

His jhola in place over his shoulder, Babu boarded a Pune-bound bus whose engine was already roaring, and occupied a window seat.

The bus stopped for a moment in front of the chai shack, to enable the driver to pay the shack owner some dues. Babu saw a young scavenger girl, with her baby strapped on her back, holding a broom in each hand, sweeping the shop front with both brooms. She had covered her nose and mouth with her dupatta, so as not to breathe in the dust she was clearing away.

This is Lakshmibai, the Rani of Jhansi, Babu thought. The thought seemed to have communicated itself to the scavenger queen. She turned around and dropped her dupatta and looked at Babu. The same oval head, broad chin, strong, long limbs, diamond-dotted nose. And as the bus started again, Jnaneshvari widened her eyes and there was a simultaneous sideward movement of her mouth.

Babu closed his eyes and offered a namaskara to Muniya-Jnaneshvari's casteless omnipresence.

Babu took an autorickshaw home from the bus station in Pune. He had anticipated that he wouldn't be able to return from Alandi until quite late in the evening and had urged Arun, ignoring his and Archana's protests, not to receive him at the bus station. It was close to midnight when he reached his ashrama, Muniyashrama, as he thought of it.

The children and Arun were asleep. Archana was up and heated the khicchri (Babu's favourite food) she had cooked for him, which Babu ate in the kitchen and later helped Archana wash dishes as he recounted the highlights of his pilgrimage, including the chai shack interrogation. But he did not reveal to Archana the dream and daylight manifestations of the mystery woman, very possibly a privileged prevision of Muniya's grown up form, a gift of Jnaneshvari, which had stirred him to the depths of his being.

Archana and Babu were both tired and said goodnight with a 'more later' expression of apology and anticipation in their eyes.

Babu was restless inside his mosquito tent. He wanted the momentum of his sacred journey (the lion-roaring of the bus, diesel-vehicle of Durga, whose images decorated the driver's cabin) to bring some concluding insight before sleep. And the insight did come, a very painterly set of animated images, condensed thought not dream, during the twilight moments between drowsiness and sleep.

A vast crowd had gathered around the Statue of Liberty in New York, at the centre of which, and looking towards the skyscraping, torch-bearing, crowned head of Goddess Liberty was Svami Vivekananda. And Vivekananda then raised both arms in salutation to the Goddess of European Enlightenment, anonymous and famous (from Plato to Marx) humanity joining him in this gesture which looked like the unexamined acceptance of the goals of modernity by the whole world.

And then the metamorphosis, a miracle of transmutation inaugurating a new-age of integral spirituality and secular responsibility.

Babu saw the Statue of Liberty coming alive, becoming invisible, and then resurrecting itself as a tall brown girl with her strong, long arms swaying in improvised devotional dance. Amazingly, she sought out Babu who was flat on his back in his bed. The crowd had vanished. She stood on Babu's chest, as Kali does on Shiva's in sacred iconography, but weightlessly. And as she lowered her head to look at Babu, her wild black hair fell all over her shoulders like sudden rainfall, and Babu received her gracious smile of amused acceptance: eyes widening, and a simultaneous sideward movement of the mouth. She was the scavenger-queen, Muniya's future form.

And then Jnaneshvari disappeared, and the entire scene with her.

Deep in his heart, like a telephone call, Babu heard an unfamiliar feminine voice, and the mantra it intoned: 'tat tvam asi'.

You are that, all things and nothingness.

That was the teaching of Sri Krishna. And Jnaneshvara Maharaj's communication of that teaching to an assembly of scholars which is his great commentary on the Gita.

Muniya's summons to Babu to sadhana which would enable him to teach that truth to her years later.

'Ramana, let me not fail Muniya!' With this prayer, Babu ended his day of pilgrimage and slept.

Iconography

Call it coincidence or cosmic conspiracy, but at breakfast in the morning after the revelatory and restful course of the night before, Arun confronted him with a question precisely about Kali dancing on the chest of a prostrate Shiva!

'Ravi, isn't the Gita about Krishna resurrecting the unexpectedly extinguished destructive fervour of Arjuna, the great Pandava warrior?' Arun asked militarily, biting off a large chunk of apple and chewing it vigorously. Babu looked at the decorated former squadron leader with understanding, but before he could say anything in response to that poser, Arun resumed his questioning, his words spaced out because the chewing was not yet complete.

'Ravi, it has just occurred to me that the popular and powerful but challenging image of Kali dancing on the chest of a prostrate Shiva ceases to be a conundrum if one remembers that Shiva is the divinity of destruction, and for some mysterious reason has allowed his destructive powers to become somnambulant, and Kali, like Krishna in relation to Arjuna's despondency in the Gita, is kick-starting those powers!' Thus, brilliantly, Arun concluded his inquiry.

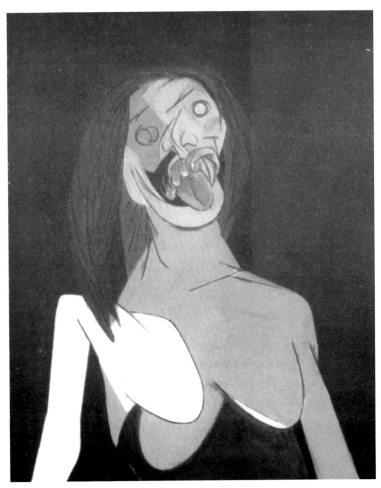

Kali's Head, Tyeb Mehta, 1996, Acrylic on Canvas, 75 x 61 cm

Archana and Babu looked at each other in wordless acknowledgement of the incisiveness of that piece of lateral thinking. It was an all-adult dining table, Muniya and Abhinava after being fed had been sent off outside to play in the courtyard with Kalpana. Without the distraction of Muniya's presence and poise, and the disturbance of Abhinava's crying, Babu was able to concentrate on Arun's thought-provoking words for a full two minutes without uttering a word. But at the end of that period of contemplation, he shook his head with professorial energy.

'My dear Arun,' he said, 'I think your thought is vehemently interesting but not convincing. Arjuna in the beginning of the Gita has not only lost the destructive fervour of a warrior going into battle, he has lost the will to live, the sense of the worthwhileness of his life has deserted him. He is in the grip of the falsehood, "I am only this body", which causes him in anguish to see all, even kinsmen, as "others"; and of the falsehood "I am not this body at all", which leaves him in despair, ready to renounce the world and even to die without resistance at the hands of the Kauravas.

'Sri Krishna seeks to release him from this double delusion with nothing less than the upanishadic power and range of the teaching of the Gita, he does not merely try and revive Arjuna's temporarily dampened warrior impulses.

'Kali dancing on the prostrate form of Shiva is not a representation of Arjuna's distress and Krishna's determination to end it. It is a portrayal of the teaching of the Gita itself. The composite image conveys the truth that the play of life and death, the drama of self's ceaseless self-imaging, can only manifest on the foundation of unflappable self-realisation.

'The erotic and sociological inversion inherent in the iconography, which makes Kali an active partner in the play of love, and Shiva the subjugated partner in the distorted life of dualism, is an invitation and a provocation to see the truth of Advaita in its full glory.'

It was Arun and Archana's turn to look at each other in admiration of the clarifying character of Babu's response.

'Where are you, Muniya?' is all that Babu wanted to say.

Babu seemed disheartened as there was no response from Muniya to his call. Arun buried himself in the morning newspaper, but Archana had noticed Babu's disappointment and brought him a fresh glass of hot tea and consoled him with the information that throughout the previous day, when Babu was away, Muniya had been hard at work with her crayons and sketchbook, making figures that looked like rectangular samadhi slabs and walls, and at least one broom-like figure, her artistic labour punctuated by chanting which included a sound like 'tatumsi, tatumsi'. Had he taught her the 'tat tvam asi' chant too?

'This is unbelievable!' exclaimed Babu, awestruck by the realisation that the 'tat tvam asi' mantra must have been received by Muniya from the depths of her own being. 'Muniya!' he called again, more pleadingly than before, but once again there was silence. But Babu quickly understood that the mantra was demanding his own attention, and would not serve as a summons to a supposed 'other', however beloved.

Noticing the transformation of Babu's bearing from anxiety to acceptance, Archana ventured the hypothesis that Muniya's company would have to be sought by a more tranquillised Babu.

'However, while the engines of iconographical understanding are roaring away in your mind, would you address a question about the Kali-standing-on-Shiva image which I have heard raised in feminist circles?' Archana asked Babu. Arun laid aside his newspaper, and smiled at Babu, urging Archana to confront him with the feminist query.

'I have heard it said with indignation,' Archana resumed. 'That the icon is a protest against the Indian, especially Hindu, tradition of male celibacy, which is seen as harbouring a patriarchal fear and hatred of women, a refusal by men to acknowledge women's procreation-independent sexuality. Have you a response to that, Babu, or have I caught you unprepared, worse, unaware?'

Babu covered his face with both hands, as though he wanted to reproduce conditions more favourable to the reading of the inner meaning of sacred images, recalled the vibrant adivasi sankeertana dancer of his most recent dream, and spoke with conviction.

'Not only do Shiva and Parvati have children, theirs is an indissoluble union of non-dualist sexuality, they are one being, flesh, substantiality, throbbing with the ceaseless orgasm of self-realisation: aham, aham, aham ....

'But you have made me curious about something. Something crucial for our country and Indian, especially Hindu, spirituality to come to terms with in our age,' Babu confessed.

'Could it be that the icon prophetically draws attention to Hinduism's failure to communicate its deepest, most integral, wisdom to the world at large without the suspect mediation of missionary translations and orientalist trivialisations? Could the icon be clamouring for the dawn of the age of Ramakrishna and Vivekananda, Ramana, Aurobindo and Gandhi?' Babu concluded, breathless with what sounded, especially to his former university contemporary, Arun, like undergraduate enthusiasm. And as a postscript, Babu added, 'Hinduism is not, and need not, be a proselytising faith. But it could be more communicative.'

Muniya came running into the dining room with her sketchbook and spread it open on Babu's lap, as if to suggest that her supportive sketchwork during Babu's pilgrimage might contain an answer to his question.

Not wanting to disturb Babu and Muniya in their collaborative divination of the meaning of her sketchbook doodlings, Archana disappeared into the kitchen and Arun sought a chair in the veranda to read the rest of the newspaper, the ritual exercise interrupted by early morning iconographical speculations.

Babu put on and then pushed his reading glasses up from his eyes to his forehead, something he always did when he had to look at serious art-work, and placed Muniya's sketchbook on the dining table and turned over its recently inscribed pages.

Yes, there were the samadhi-like structures which Archana had mentioned. These could, of course, have been images of the Alandi samadhi of Jnaneshvara Maharaj psychically received by Muniya. And the broom-like forms too, could have been transmitted to her by her scavenger look-alike outside the chai shack.

More prosaically, the samadhi forms could have been inspired by the tomb of a Muslim air force colleague of Arun's (shot down in the 1971 war) in the nearby burial ground on which Arun placed a memorial wreath of flowers every year, and would often be accompanied by the entire family in this ritual tribute.

And the broom-forms by Kalpana's brooms?

As Babu debated these possibilities in his mind, humming the lyrics of the Hindi film song, 'Tujhe khushi mile itni ke man mein na samaye, khushbu teri aisi, madhuban mein na samaye ...,' and monitored Muniya's reactions to these inquiries. She kept staring at his forehead, perhaps wondering if he had sufficient third-eye insightfulness to divine her doodling script.

Turning another page, Babu saw rows upon rows of bead-like formations, surely indicative of a sacred necklace, mangalasutra, like the one her Ayi wore round her neck, a woman's assurance that her buddhi and senses were adorned by the encompassing light of self-awareness.

'Babygirl, Muniya meri, I have to tell you a Ramana Maharshi story, the story of the missing mala or necklace,' Babu announced, and lifted Muniya on to his lap, and with all seriousness of upanishadic, secret, hushed speaking, he let the story tell itself:

'Muniya, gudiya, a woman thought she had lost her mala, her mangalasutra, the necklace of self-awareness, a thought which broke her heart!

'She looked for the mala in her kitchen, in her bedroom, in the market-place, and in the nearby forest where she often went to play with celestial beings who lived there!

'But she could not find her mala!

'Dejected (Muniya narrowed her eyes in compassion as Babu uttered this sad word), she walked all the way to the village temple and sat down on the steps of the temple tank. And washed her tired face with the sacred water, and then, because she could not hold her tears back, she closed her eyes. (Babu also closed his eyes as he related this detail and saw from a corner of his right eye that Muniya had also closed her eyes, properly, without spying with a corner of either eye!)

'And then she opened her eyes, straightened her long dark hair and tied it into a defiant jooda (knot) and looked down again into the tank waters, which had by this time become still and clear like a mirror.

'And what did she see there, Muniya? Her necklace hanging round her neck! She hadn't lost it at all, it had merely slipped around her neck and got entangled in her hair, and could not easily be touched or seen. Or, perhaps, a naughty celestial being who had stolen her mala had restored it to its proper place round the neck of the distraught but beautiful woman. (Muniya's eyes moved ever so slightly to acknowledge this possibility, without committing herself entirely to the miracle.)

'Rather like your speaking capabilities which Baba and Ayi thought you had lost, but you hadn't really!

'You had only lent them to Babu in distant Tiruvannamalai to help him with his sadhana.

And when you caught his eye and recognised him as an ancient companion with your initiating smile, his guru, Sri Ramana, restored your shakti of speech back to you!'

'As Babu's mala story ended, he looked at Muniya hoping to be blessed yet again (greedy Babu!) with her trademark smile, but instead of doing him that favour, the little girl pulled off his reading glasses from his forehead, jumped off his lap and ran out of the dining room shrieking with laughter!

'Muniya, naughty girl, come back! Muniya, come back!' Babu shouted and ran in pursuit.

Putting on his glasses for myopia, Babu walked out of the dining room and sat on the topmost step of the veranda (steps are for sitting down, not climbing up or down, thought Babu, philosophically non-partisanly), and refused to respond to Muniya's wave of her little hands inviting him to chase her and retrieve his reading glasses which were now perched on her forehead. Not because he wouldn't have enjoyed the chasing game, but because it occurred to him that Muniya had taught him an important spiritual truth, and not only provided him with an opthalmological variation of Ramana's Vedantic story of 'the missing mala'. He waved his arms above his head in a gesture of surrender, which Muniya celebrated by breaking into pirouettes.

The noise of Muniya's giggling flight and Babu's wailing appeal to her to return the glasses caused Archana to come out into the veranda and sit down next to Babu, and even Arun sitting in the corner let his newspaper slide down to the floor, and all three were entranced by Ananya's dance of devotion and mischief. Even Abhinava, watching from his special vantage position in Kalpana's arms, clapped.

Babu thought yakshaganas (celestial dancers and musicians and witnesses of all happenings of spiritual import) had manifested in the sky above the courtyard to watch this spectacle of a little girl's Krishna-like pranks, compelling joyous contemplation, not adult indignation.

Babu spoke in hushed tones of pauranika comprehension.

'Arun, Archana, by Guru's grace I can see that we are being reminded by and through Muniya that adults in our age have forgotten that to see and understand what is close to us, we do not need external instruments like reading glasses and go into a panic when we misplace them.

'Our inner eye (like Shiva's), iconographically located on our forehead like my reading glasses are now on Muniya's wide, luminous, "matha", is undetachable from us. It is self's ceaseless self-awareness, self-certainty, our closest vision of what is closest to us, ourselves.

'As I think I mentioned in my letter to you from Tiruvannamalai before leaving for Pune, the most lucid image of this self-certainty, this deliverance of our inner "reading glasses", is the condition of childhood, about which alone, and not anything else in our lives, we are absolutely certain about, that is, that we are or have been children.

'And because along with our certitude regarding our childhood, we are also aware of that childhood being nurtured, however imperfectly, by a woman, our mother, or some other woman, the image which peerlessly represents the certitude of self-awareness is that of a girl-child, for example, Muniya, dancing away right there in front of us. Like Kali, yes, dear Arun and Archana, like Kali. And I want to offer yet another reading of the Kali-dancing-on-Shiva icon we have been talking about.'

Arun and Archana were intrigued and urged Babu to continue with his labour of pauranika divination.

'The cruelties that are heaped upon the girl-child in India (exclusive preference and prayers for male progeny being the root cruelty), by nearly all communities, is unethical in the extreme, of course, but it is also dangerous self-forgetfulness. Forgetfulness of the symbolic and substantial connection between self-awareness and its most lucid self-image in our lives.

'I fear that in the near future, with advances in medical technology making it possible to determine the gender of the foetus, an era of selective female foeticide will commence.

'Kali dancing her mad dance of destruction on a prostrate Shiva is also a dark prophecy of the girl-child, manifested on the foundation of Shiva's, self's, equipoise of being, assuming the form of an all-devouring disharmony within nurturing, feminine, nature, and annihilating all life on earth, should we fail to match the self-certainty of self-awareness with love and respect for its luminous form.'

Abhinava had stopped clapping as Babu concluded his terrifying reading of the episode of his misplaced reading glasses, and Muniya's hijacking of them. Muniya froze in her sankeertana, the reading glasses falling off her forehead, redundant as they are for an enlightened being, and walked slowly towards the veranda steps and climbed up to where Babu was sitting, now with his hands covering his eyes in terror and shame.

And then, with the compassion of a Jnaneshvari, Muniya took out a red crayon hidden in her frock, and made a round bindi on Babu's forehead, returning his inner eye to him, and joined everybody in redemptive laughter.

Kalpana returned the reading glasses to Babu.

Indian Indivisibility

Evening radio news on 31 October 1983 confirmed the point-blank shooting of Prime Minister Indira Gandhi by two Sikh bodyguards from her special security force earlier during the day. The shooting had been reported in afternoon announcements, but news of her death was broadcast only in the evening, presumably to enable police and paramilitary forces throughout the country to mobilise themselves to quell possible anti-Sikh riots.

The following days revealed how ineffective the mobilisation was, as news poured in of the slaughter of hundreds of innocent Sikhs – men, women and children – who had nothing to do with the assassination of Indira Gandhi or the movement for a secessionist Sikh state – by vengeful mobs, especially in Delhi, with the apparent connivance or encouragement of the machinery of the state.

Arun was in close touch with his contacts in the armed forces and was relieved to learn that desertion from the forces by Sikh soldiers had been minimal and ended quickly, but every day he and Archana brought news of growing Hindu resentment against Sikhs in the country, and of the feeling among many Sikhs – and not only Sikhs – that Indira had invited her own assassination by ordering the army to attack the holiest of Sikh shrines, the Golden Temple in Amritsar, although no one could deny that the shrine had been converted into a fortress of secessionism by the charismatic Sikh cleric Jarnail Singh Bhindranwale. Orders would be sent out from the Golden Temple by Bhindranwale for the murder of Hindus throughout Punjab, and the murderers allowed sanctuary in the shrine.

Babu shared Arun's and Archana's sense of outrage at the murder of an unarmed woman by her bodyguards, although he had been an open critic of the tyranny Indira Gandhi had imposed upon the country in 1975 in the name of a 'national emergency', narrowly escaping imprisonment. And, like them, he also regarded the idea of another partition of the country on religious lines as abhorrent and wholly avoidable.

But he would not talk for days, retreating to his room to meditate and pray to Ramana Maharshi for a deeper understanding of what had happened which would reveal the significance of the integrity of India for the modern world as a whole, and for the future of life and civilisation on earth.

Arun and Archana found him sobbing in his bed one afternoon, asking a strongly silent Muniya who sat next to him, with her little left palm on his forehead, 'Why, Muniya, why?' Why didn't Gandhi visit Tiruvannamalai in 1946 for Sri Ramana's darshana? Surely the sage would have blessed him with power to prevent the vivisection of our motherland!' Muniya would say nothing, not even 'Aum', but she would not leave him until he looked more reconciled within himself.

It occurred to Arun that one way of drawing Babu more fully into reflection and debate on the large questions raised by the assassination of Indira Gandhi was to let a British scholar he knew, a political scientist who was currently a visiting professor at the University of Pune, interview him, something the scholar had expressed a desire to do, but a matter Arun, knowing Babu's reserve, had hesitated to pursue.

Arun now confronted Babu with a fait accompli.

'Ravi, Mark Smith, a familiar figure at my club, is joining us for lunch tomorrow. He might ask you some questions about the possibility and desirability of the indivisibility of India. I hope you won't, like Arjuna, want to run away from battle!'

'How can I do that after my darshana of Jnaneshvari at Alandi?' was Babu's answer, his gaze fixed on Muniya's face, his smile imitating hers.

Arun persuaded Ravi to join him for an evening at the Pune Club to take their minds off temporarily from the enormity of the tragedy that had befallen the country, predictable though it was, given the shortsightedness and visionlessness of Indian politics. And also to let Babu unwind before the interview with Mark Smith over lunch at home the next day. An encounter which Arun feared could be explosive, given the opportunity which the Amritsar catastrophe would provide Smith for saying 'We told you so,' echoing Churchill's grim prophecy of the chaos he thought would follow British withdrawal from India. And the patriotic and philosophical, but not necessarily polite, counter-offensive which such provocation would invite from Babu.

During the long ride to Arun's club, Babu had hummed (with Arun joining him somewhat sceptically) the integrationist Raj Kapoor song 'Meera juta hai japani, ye patloon englistani, sar pe lal topi rusi, phir bhi dil hai Hindustani ...,' establishing his liberal credentials beyond doubt. And he had recalled an amazing, Britain-celebrating episode from his long years in Britain as a student of modern Anglo-American philosophy.

Babu recalled a summer vacation in Oxford, where he spent most of his time at the Bodleian Library, reading memoirs of dons which included accounts of their encounter with Gandhi during the latter's brief visit in 1934 to the university. Apparently, at lunch at Balliol, his hosts asked Gandhi what he would like to eat. 'Hot water and salt, please!' had been his eccentric request, which was immediately complied with by the unflappable islanders. Babu nearly choked as he laughingly explained to Arun the symbolism of that request: the British Empire had found itself in a lot of hot water during Gandhi's 'salt' march a couple of years earlier!

During his stay in Britain, Babu had discovered the warmth and poverty of working people in that country, and not only their racism which was but a crude, ego-boosting, imitation of the subtler antipathy practiced by the privileged sections of British society. And so, not surprisingly, Babu frequented a café in Oxford in St Giles Square (not far from the Bodleian Library), where a lot of working people congregated for cheap meals and hot cups of tea. The café had swing-doors and was run by a strong northern woman whom all, including Babu, called 'Mum'.

'It was late summer afternoon, but still luminous, somewhat in the way post-imperialist Britain so often managed to be, for example, in the magical music of the Beatles. Indeed, the café jukebox was playing the haunting Beatles' number 'I want to hold your hand'.

'I was sitting close to the counter, chatting animatedly with Mum, the one-sidedness of the conversation compensated by Mum's concentrated attention. The café hummed with happy laughter. Everything seemed congruent with the Beatle's song of love.

'And then, Arun,' Babu continued, in a suddenly lowered tone of voice and with anguish. 'The café doors swung open, and two young men with heavily bandaged arms walked in, sheepishly, not daringly, as in Hollywood Westerns. But quite as in those films, the café now fell totally silent, and somebody switched off the jukebox.

'Anything could have happened. The young men could have come in looking for enemies: whites or wogs or nigs. But they averted Mum's eye and stood rooted near the door, which continued to swing for a while. When the doors stopped swinging and were still, matching the contrite stillness of the wounded warriors of the street, Mum's voice was heard loud and clear and canonically Yorkshire in its deadpan judgement:

'Who won?' is all she asked, and ordered the jukebox to be switched on again.

'Arun, ahimsa is a rare plant, but it does not grow in India alone,' Babu concluded, and tried to hum the difficult tune of the Beatles' song – 'I want to hold your hand'. Recalling Mum's face and voice and the miracle of reconciliation she had wrought in a little known café long ago in a distant land was less difficult.

From their corner in the large lounge of the club, Arun drew Babu's attention to Mark Smith entering with an Indian companion, neither of them in bandages.

'Do you want to talk to him now?' Arun asked Babu.

'No, tomorrow, after I have held Muniya's hand,' was Babu's emphatic reply.

It was noon when Babu returned from a stroll, in time for the lunch interview with Mark Smith, who was expected to make his appearance around 12.30 p.m.

The lunch was going to be an all-adult affair. Muniya and Abhinava had already been fed and were in the garden at the back of the house where Kalpana was hanging out laundry.

Muniya sat on the grass with her baby brother and tried to tell him the story Babu had told her about the woman who thought she had lost her mala, confident that he would grasp its meaning despite his limited vocabulary (Abhinava was two years old).

Kalpana noticed that in her conversation with Abhinava, Muniya managed to look exactly like Babu when he told her stories or discussed philosophical matters with the absolute confidence of being understood by her.

Meanwhile Arun and Babu sat down on cane chairs in the veranda, Babu on a straightbacked one to suit his rheumatic back, and waited for Mark Smith.

Two more chairs had been brought out into the veranda, the one next to Babu for Smith, and the one next to Arun, and closer to the dining room, for Archana.

In the courtyard outside a game of kabaddi was in progress.

Boys from neighbouring homes, including children of domestic staff, formed the two teams.

Babu was about to launch into an interpretation of the meaning of the game of kabaddi, but Arun urged him to concentrate his thoughts on questions of Indian sovereignty and the vulnerability of the Indian nation to communal fragmentation, matters on which he was quite certain Mark Smith would question Ravi relentlessly.

Precisely at 12.30 p.m. a taxi rolled into the Kulkarni courtyard, scattering the kabaddi players like a horde of pigeons, and stopped in front of the veranda.

Mark Smith stepped out of the vehicle unaided by the taxi driver, and stood at the bottom of the veranda steps with outstretched arms.

'Good afternoon, Arun, I hope I am not late,' he said affably, and Arun greeted him with equal fervour and assured him that he was punctual as only the British could be. Walking down the steps briskly, Arun shook hands with Smith militarily, escorted him up the steps to the veranda and introduced him to Babu, and Babu to him, with unfussy brevity:

'Professor Mark Smith, Professor Ravi Srivastava.'

Babu held out his hand for a handshake, but the visitor folded his hands in a namaste, and then each tried to do the opposite thing at the same time and this caused Arun to laugh and the two professors to snigger sophisticatedly.

Arun, the perfect host, joked about this, saying, 'East is now West, and West is East, and yet the two will surely prove Kipling right by still not meeting!' and led Mark to the chair next to Babu's, adding that Archana was busy in the kitchen and would join them soon.

Smith lowered himself into the cane chair with practised ease (he had been a frequent visitor to India) and announced that he was a vegetarian and expressed the hope that Archana had not taken the trouble to cook any non-vegetarian food. Heaving a sigh of relief when Arun informed him that everybody in the house was a vegetarian, Smith lit a cigarette and looked around for an ashtray. Arun went inside the house in search of one.

'Professor Smith, you are a vegetarian, how can you also be a smoker?' Babu asked, with affected seriousness, which caused Smith to become immediately suspicious of Ravi Srivastava's goodwill towards him.

'Srivastava, I mean Professor Srivastava, are you suggesting that there is animal flesh in tobacco?'

Arun heard this explosive beginning of the interview as he returned to his chair with an ashtray, which he placed on the floor near Smith.

'Of course not, Professor Smith, I am aware that there is no animal product in tobacco. But I imagine your being a vegetarian has something to do with your not wanting to hurt animal life?'

'Of course it does!' Smith snarled, drawing a deep puff on his cigarette.

'But you are an animal, aren't you, Professor Smith, and your smoking must hurt you, violating the foundation of vegetarianism,' Babu asserted in a very deadpan British way. It was a British friend who had confronted the vegetarian Ravi with this argument during his smoking days as a student in Britain, and Ravi had merely wanted to pull Smith's leg a bit.

But Smith was not expecting British humour from Srivastava, and exploded in anger.

'Srivastava, you wish to deny me ordinary humanity! I always suspected Indian patriotism to be deeply racist!' Smith muttered and put out his cigarette in disgust.

Arun sat there uninterferingly, but anxiously, not knowing what was going to come next in the way of Indo-British relations.

'My dear Smith,' Ravi retorted in a patronising English way, 'We human beings are not superior to animals but an inferior species, merely, of animal life, because we alone kill beyond the necessities of survival. I have always suspected that modern western humanism has become a form of species-racism, now that the older variety of racism is without any real takers even in the West!'

Arun intervened and hustled Mark Smith into the dining room, leaving Babu to meditate on what had happened to British humour.

And Archana, who had been listening to the conversation standing at the veranda door, came up to Babu and literally pulled his ears (as she would Muniya's, a thought which pleased Babu immensely) and led him also to the dining room, as lunch had been laid out.

'Atithi devo bhava,' she reminded Ravi, that is, a guest has the status of a god.

Under normal circumstances, Archana would have asked Babu to chant an invocatory mantra before proceeding to serve rice and dal and vegetables to Mark Smith, letting Arun and Babu help themselves. But she did the ritual service for the special guest straightaway. Any sort of Hindu chanting that afternoon would have made Smith feel that he was being pointedly reminded of his foreignness. She exchanged a quick glance with Babu and his silent nod of the head with closed eyes assured her that he understood the reason for the emergency omission of any invocatory prayer before the meal.

Smith ate with his fingers with exhibitionist zeal, and then, turning suddenly away from the chatter of preliminary conversation, asked Babu a pointed question.

'Professor Srivastava,' he asked, 'Aren't Hindus and Muslims and Sikhs culturally and racially and religiously sufficiently different from one another to make the Muslim and Sikh desire for separate sovereignties in the erstwhile Indian subcontinent a perfectly natural aspiration?'

Babu's reaction was quick and sharp. 'Now, now, Professor Smith, if that were so, why are all Hindus and Muslim and Sikh immigrants from the subcontinent in Britain called wogs, without any fine-tuning of derogatoriness?'

War had resumed, and Arun and Archana let it take its course.

'Now, now, Srivastava, I mean Professor Srivastava, you are talking about the undifferentiating incompetence of the working classes in Britain. Scientific, sophisticated, cultural anthropology documented the marked differences between Hindus, Muslims and Sikhs, ages ago.'

'Don't evade my question, play fair!'

'Let us indeed,' concurred Babu, and went on to point out that Mr Jinnah, the founder of Pakistan, had spelled out these alleged differences very clearly, especially between Hindus and Muslims, but that on each count he had been wrong, never mind whatever support he derived from sophisticated, scientific, cultural anthropology.

'Professor Smith, Jinnah claimed that Hindus and Muslims professed different faiths. In this he was of course factually right, but he failed to realise that this difference only showed that both communities took religion seriously in the modern world, unlike others, for example, the British.

'And Jinnah again factually correctly pointed out that Hindus and Muslims had different food prohibitions, forgetting, again, that this only indicated that they took food prohibitions seriously in a world which was becoming increasingly indifferent to what it ate, so long as it was junk food.

'And Jinnah emphasised that Hindus and Muslims dressed differently for worship, quite correctly factually to a certain extent, but again, forgetting that this only highlighted the uniting, and not dividing, fact that they took the matter of dressing for worship seriously!

'And again, but this time even factually fallaciously, Jinnah claimed that Hindus and Muslims spoke different languages. All Muslims, and not only Muslims, in the subcontinent speak or understand Urdu, but they also speak beautifully the languages of their cultural regions, Gujarati or Marathi or Punjabi or Bengali or Tamil or Telugu or Malayalam or whatever.

'Professor Smith, if only the last Viceroy of India, Lord Mountbatten, had spoken in Urdu or Hindi to the people of India, with Gandhi by his side, and declared that the country could be divided only over his and Gandhiji's dead bodies, the demand for the vivisection of India would have disappeared overnight.

'And indeed, the splitting up of India on allegedly religious grounds did precipitate the murder of Gandhi. And didn't Mountbatten also succumb to an attack by Irish unificationists?'

That was the end of the lunch party. Professor Mark Smith got up and left abruptly, saying that he had made a great mistake in wanting to interview a diehard racist ....

This drew from Babu a sharp but quiet retort as Smith hastened down the veranda steps ....

'British rule in India was institutionalised racism. In asking that racism to quit India in 1942, India awakened the conscience of Britain and enabled her to fight Hitler's racism with a new determination. The British are supposed to be good losers. So I hope you will concede that the prestige of racism was undermined by India first, and not by Britain and her allies, in the war against fascism.'

But Professor Mark Smith was in no mood for further discussion and boarded his taxi, lit a cigarette and sped away, again disrupting the game of kabaddi.

Kabaddi

Babu urged the kabaddi players to resume their game as soon as the dust raised by the spoilsport taxi had settled, but asked them if they would like him to explore with them the deeper meaning of the game first. All team members rushed to the veranda and sat down on the floor, eager to be enlightened about the symbolism of what they had regarded as a humble rural sport, lacking the glamour of modern games like cricket, hockey and football.

Babu sat down on the floor too, supporting his rheumatic back against the stone wall, and was soon joined by Arun and Archana in solidarity. They had been deeply disturbed by the altercation between Mark Smith and Babu, and were hardly amused by Smith's allegations of racism against Babu and Indian patriotism. Kalpana with Abhinava in her arms came running with Muniya trailing behind her, and joined the sabha.

Muniya edged her way to a place next to Babu, assuming chairmanship. With her chant 'Aum tatumsi, Aum tatumsi', Babu delivered a sermon:

'Beloved children, Sri Ramakrishna Paramahamsa was once asked if God ever laughed. Of course he does, the sage replied.

When two brothers draw a line on the ground and one of them says, "The land on this side of the line is mine", and the other says, "The land on this side of the line is mine", God laughs. Because he knows that the dividing line is not going to be respected by the brothers, and because the land doesn't belong to them or anybody else, but to Gopala, God.

'Kabaddi is a game invented by Sri Krishna to transform the tragedy of separation into partnership, but who listens to him? (Babu caught Arun's and Archana's eyes in instantaneously shared understanding of the vivisection of India, the theme of Babu's aborted discussion with Smith).

'Dhritarashtra's and Duryodhana's stubbornness and greed had caused a dividing line to be drawn between the Kauravas and the Pandavas, who were first cousins. The battle-line across which they and their armies would come thundering down, not saying "kabaddi kabaddi kabaddi", but "kill, kill, kill!" Kurukshetra was going to happen.

'In a last desperate bid to prevent war, Krishna crossed the dividing line and went to the court of Dhritarashtra and taught the old blind king the game of kabaddi.

'Let not Yudhishthira and his brothers come to your court saying "kabaddi kabaddi kabaddi", breathing out air, not breathing in the air of your court, merely wanting to touch you and go back to their secure, but narrow, identity as the adversaries of your children.

'Noble King, hold the Pandavas in your arms when they come. Ask them to breathe in the air of your love for them, which is equal to your love for your own sons.

'Tell them that they are welcome to rush back to their side of the battle line and their exclusive identity. But invite them to stay with you in Hastinapura, and in partnership with your sons to assume a much bigger identity. Not only the Kaurava identity, but the vaster identity of Atman and Brahman, identity with all that *is*, and with nothingness too, with the earth and the sky.

'Let this wider, deeper, game of kabaddi be inaugurated by you, Dhritarashtra. Or else the slaughter of war awaits all.

'Children, Dhritarashtra spurned the game of kabaddi. You must understand its spirit. India must not forget its meaning. When somebody crosses a line of division, of caste or class or gender or creed, breathing out foul air and refusing to breathe in the pure air of the all-encompassing sky which unites all in the most intimate bond of identity, the identity of self-realisation, the sky under which alone this land of Bharata has most insistently sought to live, we must hold them, not in imprisonment, but in the embrace of the reminder that we are not "self and other", that all are self-images of singular selfhood. All are images of Muniya!'

Muniya blessed the sabha with her trademark eyes-and-mouth movement, and Babu resumed his sermon, newly empowered.

'So, children, you cannot lose in kabaddi. Either you win by retaining your narrow identity. Or, by losing, you win an even greater victory, the limitless identity of self-realisation.

'Go now and play kabaddi in its true spirit. Jai Gopala!'

The sabha dispersed and the kabaddi teams resumed their engagement across the line of apparent division, their tryst with destiny, self-realisation. Kalpana took Muniya and Abhinava with her to watch the game.

'The game of kabaddi had been played for centuries in India until the British arrived and disrupted it. Caste and communal divisions were being unmasked as spiritually spurious distinctions by sages of all traditions,' Babu pointed out to Arun and Archana.

'And by drawing the spurious line of partition between Hindus and Muslims when they left, they, like Dhritarashtra, have tempted us to abandon the miracle of kabaddi in favour of the recurrent tragedy of Kurukshetra,' he concluded.

Archana pointed out that, like the British presence in India, Mark Smith's taxi had disturbed the game of kabaddi both when he came and when he left, petulantly.

'Archana and Arun, I want to share with you the instruction of a terrifying nightmare I suffered in Tiruvannamalai,' Babu confessed suddenly.

'I had been reading the Mahabharata late into the night, and stopped reading at the point when Bhishma, the great Kuru, died. As Devavrata, he had shot a circle of arrows into the everflowing Ganga, his river-mother, thereby claiming that she was the mother of the Kuru race exclusively. And he remained chained to this identity till the end.

'I recall being greatly disturbed by this example of the obstinacy of exclusivist identity, and my sleep that night surfaced a disquieting dream:

'After the death of Bhishma, and as a result of Krishna's Gita instruction to Arjuna which had been faithfully transmitted to her and her husband by Sanjaya, Gandhari was intellectually convinced that exclusivist identities, such as her husband's clinging Kuru identity, like her own Gandhara (modern Afghanistan) identity, were invitations to disaster.

'But her heart was not ready to accept a more inclusive self-definition. She dearly wanted to see her Gandhara body just once, to delight in its glory and specificity.

'In my dream I saw her stand in front of a great mirror in a private space lit by candles and disrobe herself, and also remove her blindfold. I recall her whispering to herself (she didn't want Dhritarashtra to hear what she was saying) that in looking at her mirror image she was only imitating self-awareness, not breaking her vow of visual blindness!

'It took a while for Gandhari to be able to focus on her visual image, unused as she had become to visual experience, but when she was finally able to see her yoga-honed flesh, taut breasts, the flower of desire still aflame like a fresh battle-wound, she fell in love with her Gandhara and acquired Kuru identity and dismissed Krishna's teaching as fantasy.

'I am this form, this body, this Gandhari, not everything and nothing, and will always be,' she said.

'That night Gandhari dreamt that she was the new commander-in-chief of the Kaurava army, not the low-born Karna, who merely rode her chariot.

'Gandhari saw in her dream that she fought without removing her blindfold and destroyed all the Pandavas and also Krishna, and all her sons and indeed all humanity and all life on earth. The earth itself had been destroyed and dissolved into nothingness by the violence of her exclusivist identity.

'She awoke in her dream and wanted to look at herself again in the mirror, but there was only limitless nothingness around her, everything had vanished.

'Waking up from her dream, she found herself bathed in sweat. Her husband was aroused by it and wanted to make love with her, the only time he would allow her to remove her blindfold, so she could behold his manliness.

'Gandhari removed her blindfold but instead of making love with her husband, she related her dream to him trembling in fear, begging him to make peace with the Pandavas and to accept the teaching of Krishna and liberate himself from the narrowness of his racial identity.

'The King refused to do so and Gandhari tied the blindfold round her eyes again, indifferent to the erotic prowess of her husband,' thus concluded Babu's narration of his nightmare within a nightmare.

Arun smiled as he remembered his proud Peshwa ancestors.

Archana shook her head in amazement at a sadhaka's understanding of a woman's heart.

Babu became grave. He knew he had to become a wanderer again, make a pilgrimage of study to Dakshineshvara, especially, where Sri Ramakrishna had taught the foundations of the wisdom of kabaddi, among other things.

Later, at dinner, when he made this announcement in Muniya's presence, she stopped eating and began frenziedly to draw mysterious forms in her sketchbook.

She didn't talk to Babu for days.

But on the day Babu left for Kolkata, she did. 'Aum, Babu, Muniya,' she said, as Arun's car, with Babu and his belongings in it, left for the station. The memory of Archana, Muniya, Kalpana and even Abhinava waving their hands in the English gesture of 'farewell' was to stay with Babu for years.

Temptation

Babu boarded the Deccan Queen for Mumbai from where he was to take the Howrah Mail to Kolkata, stopping over for a day in the city of dreams to see his ailing friend Tyeb Mehta (whom he had first met in Delhi), the Muslim painter whose works of Hindu iconography were unprecedented in our times in their insightfulness and reverential innovativeness. He had called up Tyeb from Arun's home in Pune, and Tyeb and his wife Sakina had asked Ravi, with great warmth, to visit them at their Juhu home.

It had not been easy to say goodbye to Arun and Archana.

'Stay with us as long as you want, Babu,' they had said the night before Babu was to leave. Babu's boyhood friend Arun, however, understood that the fireworks which had characterised Ravi Srivastava's meeting with Mark Smith would compel Ravi to set out on an outward pilgrimage (which would also be an inner journey). He would go on to seek a deeper understanding of Indian freedom, which was timelessly complete and yet always in the making, a deeper self-questioning, a forging of an armour of self-knowledge for Muniya beyond the defensiveness and petulance which had marred the movement for Indian independence from British racism.

Babu hadn't said goodbye to Muniya at all. She would know that they would always be together. Her closed mouth had trembled in its sideward movement when she came to Babu's room early in the morning (Archana had explained to her that he had to leave for Kolkata after breakfast) and found him wide-awake and sobbing. But there were no tears in her widening, radiant, prophetic eyes.

'Jai Svaraj!' the mantra with which Arun and Ravi had greeted each other when Babu arrived in Pune was also the comprehensive chant with which they said goodbye as the Deccan Queen rolled out of the station.

Leaving his luggage (the three jute bags with which he had arrived in Pune from Tiruvannamalai) in the left-luggage room at Mumbai Central, from where the Howrah Mail would depart late at night, Babu jumped on to a third-class compartment of a local train to go to Santa Cruz, from where he would take an autorickshaw to Tyeb's Juhu home.

Trapped, like Abhimanyu, in a chakravyuha of the compartment ('How would I get off at Santa Cruz?' he wondered), a strap-hanging Babu was suddenly waylaid by the temptation to release Ramana's hand which had supported him all these years. And he yielded to the temptation with the ego-sustaining thought, 'I am a philosopher, I need no support beyond reason.'

He allowed the chant 'Appa! Ramana!' which had sounded ceaselessly and silently in his mind for years, and its amplified, more recent form 'Appa! Ramana! Muniya!' to slowly but decisively recede from his consciousness.

And he looked around the compartment with what he thought were liberated, new eyes.

Through gaps between strap-hanging hands he saw a woman leper sitting at the back of the compartment, no one daring to sit next to her. She was beautiful, with a long face and broad jaw and wild hair (Jnaneshvari? No, that's impossible, Babu's liberated mind insisted). With the stump of her right hand, and widening eyes and a sideward movement of her mouth, she was daring Babu to come and sit next to her. Do you have the compassion to do so? her eyes seemed to ask. The courageous, defiant eyes of a human being who had been ostracised.

Babu turned his gaze away from her and noticed for the first time the sadhu who had been standing next to him all along, not strap-hanging but supporting himself on his own staff – the strength of orthodoxy.

'Do I have the leper woman's will to live on the margins of existence, or the sadhu's faith in the supportive power of orthodoxy in the modern world?' Babu asked himself with growing alarm.

And then, for the first time, he felt the pressure of the sozzled vagrant behind him who was leaning unembarrassedly against his back, and smelled his alcoholic breath with revulsion.

The train stopped at a station, and Babu tried to push his way out of the crowded compartment, thinking that the station was Santa Cruz, his destination.

The drunk suddenly spoke, with inexplicable knowledge of Babu's destination. This is not Santa Cruz, he said, and returned to his leaning position against Babu.

'Would I, without Ramana, and without Muniya, have this defeated, despised, drunkard's simple humanity?' Babu questioned himself ruthlessly.

And then, Babu's mind seemed to disintegrate. It was without a core of luminosity, without the power to hold disparate images in a coherent pattern, he felt he was going mad. Desperately, he let go the ceiling strap and closed his eyes and hands in obeisance to Ramana, his Guru. And prayed as follows:

'Appa! Ramana! Muniya! I can't let go of you, although I do want to question my advaitin faith ceaselessly but not without your help! Come back, please!'

His mind filled again with the silent chant 'Appa! Ramana! Muniya!' and he felt gathered again into coherence of mind and integrity of spirit.

The train stopped again. He opened his eyes. The leper woman, the sadhu and the vagrant had disappeared. He had reached Santa Cruz.

A very brief visit to Tyeb and Sakina was all that was possible, but it was a privilege for Babu to have made that pilgrimage.

Wanderings

The clanking of the wheels of the Howrah Mail reminded Babu of a jingle he had heard his father sing during train journeys from Allahabad to Delhi in his childhood: 'Chal Kalkatta dhar de paise, chal Kalkatta dhar de paise', a tune which seemed to rhyme with the crashing call of the train to progress, modernity, bankruptcy!

At one level, this theme of the rural poor being lured to the cruel city is what the large canvas, which Tyeb had shown Babu in his studio earlier in the afternoon, was all about. A recent, but a repetition of the theme of the rickshaw-puller, another work.

Reflecting on the canvas as he struggled to fall asleep (so much had happened so soon!) on his three-tier berth, Babu realised that there was no repetitiveness in the canvas at all, a new depth of meaning had been stirred by the painting beyond the portraiture of proletarian misery.

And that the work spoke of his transformed life and sadhana epitomized by the updated chant 'Appa! Ramana! Muniya!' There was too much to catch up with Tyeb and Sakina (who were also soon to visit Bengal, Tyeb had been invited to Shantiniketan as resident painter) for Babu to pay sufficient attention to the new

Rickshaw-puller, Tyeb Mehta, 1982, Oil on Canvas, 150 x 120 cm

painting, stirring and stunning though it was in its flat colouring and angled linearity like all of the painter's works.

The jingle, 'Chal Kalkatta dhar de paise', suddenly conveyed to Babu something deeper than the call of the metropolis – 'Abandon all worldly calculations, "dhar de paise", and come to Kalkatta, Kali's abode,' That was the lullaby which sent Babu to sleep.

And Tyeb's new rickshaw-puller spoke to him in a dream, identifying himself as Vivekananda.

'Babu, I know you are on your way to Kolkata to reflect on the life of my master, Sri Ramakrishna, and I, his servant, Vivekananda, welcome you to the city as a rickshaw-puller who, like hundreds of others, earns his livelihood in this capital city of a supposedly socialist state by plying a hand-pulled rickshaw.

'But I want you to understand the symbolism of this demeaning condition of ours, because it symbolises the human condition as such.

'We imagine that we pull the rickshaw of our lives with our own hands. The truth, however, as Sri Krishna explained to Arjuna in the Bhagavadgita, is that we are pushed and pulled by natural and social circumstances. Our idealistic desire to improve our circumstances is also merely a movement of natural and social causality, albeit a more worthy movement than the servility of the oppressed and the hard-heartedness of the oppressors. However, it is the omnipotent and omnipresent light of self-realisation which alone can improve the circumstances of our lives.

'In the light of self-realisation alone can we see that our bodily and mental and social circumstances are but self-images, dark or lucid, of ourselves, and be able to work on them and with them as artists work with their materials; non-dualistically, therefore, non-violently. We must surrender the reins of the chariots of our life to the luminosity of self-realisation, represented by Krishna in the Mahabharata, and by this Goddess who stands besides me. She is Sharada, Kali, Ramakrishna's Shakti, the Divine Mother. Seek her, if you want to find Ramakrishna.

'You will cease to be anthropocentric. Look at me, don't I look like a horse? And isn't Kali, like Krishna, singular self in all beings, the charioteer whose wish is my command, because it is also my deepest wish?'

Babu's dream now took the form of a close-up view of the luminous woman behind the hand-pulled rickshaw, which carried no passengers, as decreed by her. The hand-pulled, empty rickshaw now lucidly imaged the autonomy of self-awareness.

And the lucidity of self-awareness was an oval face and broad chin and the subtle animation of eyes and mouth.

'Jnaneshvari! Muniya!' Babu shouted, waking up fellow passengers who were not cross with him for invoking the Divine Mother in his sleep.

'Jai Durge!' they chanted, and went back to sleep.

'Chal Kalkatta dhar de paise, Chal Kalkatta dhar de paise.'

Sri Ramakrishna had traversed a variety of spiritual paths and always arrived at the same goal, the fundamental upanishadic realisation of the non-duality of Atman and Brahman, without abandoning his devotional relationship to Kali as the foundation of his spiritual life (much as Sri Ramana retained his devotional relationship to Arunachala so as to enable his teaching of self-inquiry to be seen as grounded in supreme, ego-dissolving, bhakti). Babu's pilgrimage to Dakshineshvara where Sri Ramakrishna brought the gift of a precious insight into the distinctive feature of Hinduism: its simultaneous espousal of image-worship and advaita, the riotous self-imaging diversity of selfhood and its supreme self-sufficient singularity, the two poles between which can be accommodated all the modes of worship of all religions, including, especially, the worship of the divine as formless but with qualities, which characterises the religious life of Judaism, Islam, Unitarian Christianity, Sikhism, Arya Samaj and Brahmo Samaj.

If you renounce or denounce image-worship or Advaita, you lose the distinctiveness of Hinduism, as Arya Samaj and Brahmo

Samaj did, and before them the traditions of doctrinaire Dvaita and Visistadvaita.

The simultaneous espousal of image-worship and Advaita is not a self-contradictory stance of a would-be comprehensive theology, but living unambiguous faith in the 'one' itself also being the 'many', the miracle which alone can make life worth living despite all its travails, in the way children find stories worth listening to (stories embody the same miracle of the fixity of hearers becoming the flexibility of the figures of a story) even at the end of a hard day for both themselves and their parents or elders.

Babu realised that this was the great renewal of self-understanding which Ramakrishna and Sarada and Vivekananda brought to Hinduism, a foundation without which even the struggle for India's political independence could not have succeeded, even to the extent to which it did.

Sadhakas who were political activists, albeit profoundly different in style and temperament, such as Aurobindo and Gandhi, were also deeply inspired by Sri Ramakrishna and Svami Vivekananda. Both had made pilgrimages to Dakshineshvara.

An episode in the life of Ramakrishna which made a deep impression on Babu was his psychic encounter with an English sailor during a period of his intense sadhana in the secluded Panchavati area of Dakshineshvara.

The sailor, Babu imagined, had come from his ship docked near Kolkata, representing the British Empire's pirating zeal which drove it round the world restlessly in search of loot.

Ramakrishna was firmly grounded on his seat of sadhana, seeking not to overpower the world but to be one with the limitless consciousness of which all worlds are but self-images, dark or luminous.

The sailor beckoned Ramakrishna in a way which had all the suggestiveness of a sexual solicitation.

Babu imagined the sailor saying to Ramakrishna: 'Come with

me and sail with me round the world, I'll give you all the pleasures and the riches of the world. Abandon your sadhana.'

Ramakrishna got up from his seat, his curiosity regarding all forms of the divine, helpful or testingly difficult, being irrepressible.

But seeing through the false choice that was being offered to him, between evanescent and enslaving worldly pleasure and power, on the one hand, and the unceasing and liberating joy of self-realisation, on the other, Ramakrishna prayed to Kali and asked her, symbolically, to kill the tempter, which she did.

Babu understood this story not as representing any kind of racist hatred of the English that Ramakrishna may have harboured, but his confrontation and overcoming, at a psychic level, of the temptation that India faced: the temptation of yielding to the British Empire's offer of racist governance, sacrificing svaraj and the trusteeship of the saving and universal truth of non-duality.

Babu decided that Sri Ramakrishna was India's first freedom fighter against British rule, his psychic rejection of its solicitation of India's soul for the doubtful gains of world-domination having made the struggle for Indian independence a historical possibility.

Sri Ramakrishna was, however, no racist, as is poignantly made clear by another story which Babu encountered in his careful reading of the *Ramakrishna Kathamrita*.

Ramakrishna recounted a visit of his to the Kolkata Maidan where he saw an English lad standing against a tree in Sri Krishna's 'tribhanga' pose (bent in three places), at the neck, hips, and knees, and went into samadhi!

It is the self, Atman, which 'appears' to be bent at three places: the places marked by the waking state, the dream state and the sleep state: the fourth or turiya harmony of the three states manifesting its 'Krishna' attractiveness, the beauty of the English boy Ramakrishna saw.

This is not homosexuality, manifested or sublimated, but the ecstasy of self-realisation, the incomparable orgasm of the one revealing itself as also the many.

During his years of study of the Ramakrishna-Vivekananda tradition in Kolkata and Dakshineshvara, Babu came across what struck him as a major event in the spiritual history of humanity.

In August 1898, Svami Vivekananda went on a pilgrimage to Amarnath in Kashmir. Svamiji was in poor health but he climbed the steep hill to Amarnath and at the precise moment of his entry into the cave of Shiva, he spotted pigeons, a rare occurrence which, according to local belief, confers upon the fortunate pilgrim the boon of 'icchha mrtyu', the power to die only when one wishes to.

Spurning this power, Vivekananda descended to the temple of the Divine Mother in the Kashmir Valley, the Kshira Bhavani shrine.

There he offered prescribed oblations and prayers to Kali and sat down to meditate deeply on the condition of his country and religion.

His Kayastha heart could not remain peaceful for long. He spoke his heart out to Kali.

'Mother, why did you permit the Islamic invader to come again and again and break your images and destroy your temples? Why, Mother, why did you let this happen? Had I been around, I would have protected you!'

Vivekananda has recorded that Kali answered his question, a question which continues to trouble millions of Hindus and is at the back of the Hinduism-denying vengefulness of the Ayodhya agitation for rebuilding a Rama temple allegedly destroyed by Babur in the sixteenth century.

And for the first time in recorded spiritual history, the divine, as Kali, spoke to a Hindu devotee as a voice from the sky (not from her image) in the manner of the principal revelations of the Judaic, Christian, and Islamic faiths.

She said: 'Vivekananda, what is it to you if I have permitted this to happen? Do you protect me, or do I protect you?'

Babu was enabled by Ramana's grace to understand Kali's response to Vivekananda as also addressed to Muslims, because she spoke as one without form, a voice from the sky.

She was conveying to Hindus and Muslims the deep meaning of their coexistence on the Indian subcontinent for a thousand years.

'They had both been protected, one tradition was not allowed to overwhelm the other. It was Hindus and Muslims who had failed to protect one another.

'Atoning gratitude on the part of both alone could form the basis of enduring peace in Kashmir and between the two communities.'

Records show that Vivekananda's troubled heart was at peace after the 1898 revelation. He died a few years later.

A future Bible must incorporate among its revelations a Book of Vivekananda, incorporating the formless divine's 'feminine' voice speaking to him about the divine's protection of the truth in all spiritual traditions.

Babu learned that Sri Ramakrishna had had a vision of his beloved Kali not only as stone image, vibrantly alive, worshipped by him and all devotees in her shrine at Dakshineshvara, but also as formless light which assumed all forms. And as a little girl and a young woman as real as the people around him.

'Appa, won't I see my Muniya also as a young woman, and through my love for her, won't I also see her as formless light which assumes all forms?' Babu would weep and offer this prayer to Ramana sitting in the Kali shrine at Dakshineshvara absorbed in thoughts about Ramakrishna.

And, opening his eyes, he would imagine Kali's face flashing, like lightning, with that subtle and simultaneous movement of eyes and mouth which haunted his days and nights.

Atman is self-certainty, of which childhood is an unrivalled portrait. And childhood's vulnerability is powerfully symbolic of the self-distortions Atman suffers at the hands of its impostor, ego, and it is this combination of certainty and vulnerability that is

Kali, Dakshineshvara

poignantly portrayed by the girl-child, and indeed by the vulnerable condition of womanhood in all phases of its manifestation.

In his wanderings of exploration this thought never ceased to grow deeper and clearer in Babu's heart, and he imagined this process to correspond to Muniya's growth from childhood into girlhood and young womanhood (invisible to him) in Pune and Sanawar and Delhi.

Babu speculated that although the adulthood of a woman was no less complete than the adulthood of a man, the face and voice and vulnerability and intuitiveness of childhood endured in women agelessly to serve as a mirror of selfhood to themselves and to men: and that the special attractiveness of women was possibly founded in their special mirroring of selfhood: everybody loves themselves.

And the dark thought floated into Babu's mind that the misogyny which women often encountered in men may have something to do with women's portraiture of selfhood being a cruel reminder to men of their distortion of self-awareness, a hatred often heightened and not diminished by the attractiveness of women.

Travelling south again, Babu spent two years in Pondicherry, studying the life and thought of Sri Aurobindo and Sri Mira (the 'Mother').

Sri Aurobindo was sent away to England at the age of seven by his Anglophile father, and returned at the age of twenty-one as a fiery Indian patriot. This is common knowledge. As is his deep involvement in the militant struggle for Indian independence, and his retirement from politics and immersion in world-transformative yoga.

Babu realised that what is insufficiently understood is the pain Sri Aurobindo must have suffered at the thought of the likely clinical insanity of his mother, with whom he couldn't have had the opportunity of spending much time.

Could it not be, Babu speculated, that a very young Aurobindo would have vowed in his heart to liberate motherhood from all its travails?

Mother India, first, from the self-distorting humiliation of alien rule.

And Mother Asia, later, from the neglect of her saving spiritual traditions.

And Mother Humanity from the violence of its fragmentation into narrow nationalities.

And Mother Matter, finally, from the darkness of its recesses which shunned the transformative light of self-awareness? (The light-deprived cells of his insane mother's brain?)

Couldn't Sri Aurobindo's life, work and yoga as a whole be seen as an attempt to restore to motherhood in all its dimensions its spiritual primacy, the fullness of its portraiture of sourcehood, selfhood, Atman?

And might not his honouring of Sri Mira as exemplifying the deepest and widest consciousness of yoga be as enormous an event in human spiritual history as Svami Vivekananda's auditory awareness of the formless feminine divine?

Babu had philosophical difficulties with Sri Aurobindo's relegation of Advaita Vedanta and Buddhism to a status of spiritual penultimacy, but the depth of Sri Aurobindo's devotion to the divine feminine was more than corrective of that piece of unexpected philosophical injustice.

And Babu's renewed reading of all of Gandhi's writings and pilgrimages to Delhi and Sabarmati and Wardha and Porbandar confirmed him in his view that Gandhi's life was founded on remembered childhood, its vulnerability, and the companionship of his Atman-mirroring child-wife and 'sourcehood'-exemplifying mother.

This insight brought to Babu an understanding of the 'siblinghood' Gandhi sought with all women, and not only all men, in his sadhana of truth and ahimsa and brahmacharya.

It was when Gandhi and his women associates were most vulnerable to assault and assassination in Noakhali, that they often lay down naked in celibate comradeship at night, awaiting sleep or death.

And it was with his arms resting on the shoulders of two women associates, honouring their self-mirroring form, Babu thought, that Gandhi walked to his appointment with violent death: one among the two million who perished because of the partition of India. But his women associates were untouched. Their portraiture of selfhood undenied.

During the Ayodhya agitation in 1991 to rebuild a Rama temple precisely at the spot where a sixteenth century mosque existed, allegedly built by the first Mughal emperor Babur on the ruins of an earlier Rama temple which he supposedly destroyed, the agitators demolished the mosque. However, they showed no desire to subject the Ramayana episode of Sita's banishment by Rama to a test of authenticity and acceptability.

Babu wrote a work entitled *The Testimony of Janaka*, a fictional work which sought to draw attention to the need for atonement for the banishment of Sita, if that Ramayana episode is taken to be authentic, as a precondition for building a new Rama temple in Ayodhya.

And in 1998, when India and Pakistan conducted nuclear tests, Babu wrote a tract entitled *The Third Atom Bomb*, based on his conviction that splitting the spiritual unity of India was akin to splitting the material unity of the atom which unleashed the violence of Hiroshima and Nagasaki.

Both works drew flak, from Hindu fundamentalists in India and Empire loyalists in Britain.

Arun had written supportive letters to Babu during these times of isolation.

The California Institute of Integral Studies in San Francisco invited Babu in 1999 to spend two years teaching the wisdom of modern Indian spirituality to graduate students and members of the general public.

Babu realised the enormous burden of responsibility which Svami Vivekananda had bequeathed to Indians: to communicate the insights of Indian spirituality and philosophy to the modern world directly in English, but with conviction, without the fuss of translation and mediation by western scholars who did not believe in the truth of what they translated, even when their translations from Sanskrit into English were accurate. This realisation made Babu simultaneously proud and humble.

The hospitality of the English language to Indian spiritual and philosophical ideas made Babu think more charitably of the British occupation of India than he used to.

Reality

The world is full of your faces
(SHVETASHVATARA UPANISHAD, 4.3)

Muniya's Anguish

Muniya rested a carrier bag containing three tall cardboard cylinders on the vacant aisle seat, scrolled within which were (she informed Babu) prints of Picasso's 'Guernica', Francis Bacon's 'Screaming Pope', and Munch's 'Screaming Figure on a Bridge'. An indication of her current state of mind?

Muniya had insisted on Babu taking the window seat, so he could rest his head against the wall of the aircraft while sleeping, easing the discomfort of his rheumatism about which Arun and Archana had often spoken to her.

She took the middle seat.

It was going to be a long haul to London where they would be received by Haren Desai, an expatriate Gujarati (who had been expelled from Idi Amin's Uganda years earlier and found sanctuary in London, where his diamond business had flourished beyond all expectations).

Haren Desai had sponsored a lecture by Ravi Srivastava at the Bharatiya Vidya Bhavan on 'Hinduism and Violence', and offered Babu and Muniya the hospitality of his home in London for as long as they wished to stay in the city.

Dinner ('vegetarian' for Babu and Muniya) was served as soon as the aircraft had steadied itself at a higher altitude above turbulence.

It was really only after the trays containing the remnants of their meal on unfolded tables had been cleared and the tables folded back, that Babu began talking to Muniya. She had remained unselfconsciously silent throughout the meal, but not uncommunicative, catching Babu's eye frequently with her smile which was initiatory not of conversation but communion and contemplation, and layered, Babu thought, with a shade of the scepticism with which young people seek to lighten the burden of their sorrow.

Babu asked her if he could order two glasses of red wine for them to celebrate her graduation.

Muniya, whom Babu had never seen crying as a baby, now covered her face with both her hands and wept uncontrollably, although well-behavedly softly.

Babu instinctively stroked her head with his hand and could only utter words of comfort in Hindi: 'Baby meri, kuch nahin hua hai, Babu tere saath hai, bata mujhe apne dil ki baat, bata de meri baby, ro le, ji bhar ke ro le meri gudiya!'

'Babu, don't tell Baba and Ayi what I am about to tell you, promise me you won't!'

Babu promises Muniya that he wouldn't tell Baba and Ayi what he hoped she would tell him without reservation.

'I have not graduated, Babu. I passed the written examination with good grades, but I walked out of my viva. I felt the examiners were mocking my religion!'

'Were all your viva examiners American, Muniya?' Babu asked matter-of-factly.

This caused Muniya to look at him suspiciously for a moment. She weighed in her mind, with the ideological correctness in such matters which comes so easily to the young, the possibility that Babu, a passionate Hindu like her father, might regard all or most Americans or Europeans as being prejudiced against Hinduism. She tried to read his face from left to right, top to bottom, to ascertain intuitively if this could be the case. And she took an interminable minute to do this.

The Scream (Litho), Edvard Munch, 1895

Babu recalled the child Muniya's rock-like steadiness of purpose, and rejoiced at the survival of this yogic capability in Muniya the young woman, and submitted cheerfully to her psychic scrutiny of his face.

'Babu, no, one of my viva examiners was an Indian with a psychoanalytical orientation. I could sense that the questions that I was being asked were hostile.' Muniya looked carefully at Babu's face to make sure that he knew that in American academic usage, 'hostile' meant 'tough', and not, as in British usage, 'ill-wishing'. Babu's smile reassured her that he was aware of the American usage, and also that he couldn't possibly regard all American or European appraisals of Hinduism as being prejudiced. 'I felt strongly that it was in a mocking tone of voice that the questions were being fired at me,' confessed Muniya.

She was in full flow now.

'I was asked three questions, one after another, without being given a moment's pause to reflect on their import or intent.

'The first examiner, an American free-thinking theologian, shot the first question.

'Ms Kulkarni, we are close to the first anniversary of the terrorist attack on the twin towers in New York. It's all "Maya" for Hinduism, isn't it? Illusion. Not reality, which calls for energetic intervention.

'And before I could gather my thoughts to counter that accusation, the second examiner, an American cultural anthropologist, fired the second shot.

'Ms Kulkarni, do you think Hinduism or even Hindu secularism has the cultural and political resourcefulness to resolve the age-old and increasingly violent conflict between Hinduism and Islam?'

'Babu, I felt like Karna in the Mahabharata, my chair sank into the ground like his chariot wheel, and before I could pull it out and sit straight and fight clean, the third explosion came, detonated by the psychoanalytically orientated Indian examiner.

'Ms Kulkarni, do you not think the miserable state of the girl-child in India has something fundamentally to do with the weird practice of brahmacharya, or celibacy, exalted in Hindu sacred texts and preached even today by Hindu political leaders, a practice which poorly masks a deep hatred for women?'

'At this point, and as soon as the Indian examiner lit his cigar self-congratulatorily, I walked out of the viva examination.

'But something stopped me at the door of the graduate seminar building where the viva was held. I sent a note to my examiners through one of the secretaries of the graduate studies office. I asked for three months time to think about their questions and requested a fresh viva.

'Babu, within minutes the answer came, in writing, from the chief examiner: Ms Ananya Kulkarni, your request is granted.'

'I am terribly disturbed. I will be twenty-two years old next month. I wanted to return home with my graduate degree. I don't know if in three months I'll be able to face my viva examiners again, be equipped with answers to their hostile questioning of Hinduism. Babu, can you help me understand the issues raised by my examiners better? Do you have the time?'

It was Babu's turn to cover his face with his hands in shame. He cursed himself for not having been in regular touch with Muniya all these years. Had he spent even a few weeks every year with her, he would have been able to help her gain a mature understanding of Hindu thought and spiritual traditions and practices, and she, and not her examiners, would have had the last laugh. And he realised the enormous cost not only to India but to the modern world of India's refusal to be in living contact with her spiritual and philosophical traditions.

'Muniya, before your next birthday, which is also the birth anniversary of Mahatma Gandhi, I'll help you discover within your own intuitive heart and mind all the answers you seek. Aum Sri Ramanaya Namah.'

And he asked a stewardess to bring them two glasses of red wine.

Maiya as Graduate, K.S. Radhakrishnan, Bronze, 1998

Lullaby

It was now close to sleep-time for most passengers on board the big jet flying silently through the night. Babu found himself staring at the little diamond on Muniya's nose, not being able to decide which was the more exquisite creation, the diamond or the nose. His predicament must have been writ large on his face, because Muniya looked embarrassed. Unfastening her seat belt, she slung a leather bag over her left shoulder and got up with an effortless coordination of movements, all set to walk down the aisle to the loo, urging Babu, too, to find his way to the facility before a crowd gathered outside it!

Babu watched Muniya slow-dance down the passageway with her arms raised (to ease the flow of traffic in both directions) and himself set off in the opposite direction.

Close to their conveniences, synchronicity made them both look over their shoulders and catch each others' eye: in acknowledgement, perhaps, of the communion of spirit which had not been affected by physical distance all these years.

Back in their seats, Babu and Muniya resumed conversation, unmindful of the command of dimmed lights.

'Meri Muniya! Let me tell you a story from the Mahabharata which addresses with amazing precision the philosophical issues underlying your viva examiners' anxieties about Hinduism,' Babu suggested.

'Could you please try and speak more softly?' said the woman sitting in the window seat immediately ahead of Babu, in a voice which sounded very English and peeved.

Babu's monologue which followed was the most muted he had ever delivered.

'Still scared of the British?' Muniya asked Babu.

'Dead scared!' said Babu.

'The story, Babu, hush-hush,' Muniya said, and snuggled up to him to hear it better, as she used to in Pune as a child on the jhoola which was Babu's favourite storytelling seat.

'Muniya, during the last year of their banishment, before the Kurukshetra war, the Pandava brothers were in Dvaitavana, a bleak forest.

A brahmana who lived in the same forest with his family came to them with a poignant story:

> A deer has run away with our arani sticks, the sticks with which we light the sacred fire and also our cooking fire which feeds us. The sticks got entangled in the deer horns and when we tried to remove them he ran away faster than the wind.
>
> You are kshatriyas, it is your duty to help those who are in distress. The loss of arani sticks, which make it possible to tame fire, symbolises the loss of the sacred art of taming anger, fear and desire, and bodes ill for the future of life on the earth.
>
> Please find that foolish deer and restore to us those instruments of saving self-restraint, the arani-sticks!

'Muniya, the Pandavas could not find the deer even after hours of search. Thirsty, they went one by one to look for some source of drinking water. Bhima, Arjuna, Nakula, and Sahadeva, and finally the eldest, Yudhishthira.'

A vigilant stewardess thought the old man and his young

companion were thirsty and brought them some water to drink! Thanking her, Babu and Muniya drank some water, and Babu returned to the interrupted story.

'Yudhishthira found a pool of clear water and his four brothers lying dead near its edge.

'A Yaksha's voice from the sky explained to Yudhishthira that his brothers had died because they had refused to answer his questions before touching the water of the pool which belonged to him. So would Yudhishthira if he did not answer the questions, the Yaksha warned him!'

'What were the questions, Babu, the story sounds like my viva examination!' Muniya asked impatiently.

'Yes it is! But I'll tell you the rest of the story only if you whisper, ridiculously, as I am doing,' said Babu.

'Done!' whispered Muniya.

'Three of the questions are the most profound and most relevant to your viva agony:

'What is heavier than the earth?' That is the first question.

'Yudhishthira's answer to that question is: "A mother".

'The earth is solid, substantial, but not self-supporting.

'A mother, a grown-up girl-child, or any girl-child, is the very image of Atman, self-supporting self-awareness, the very meaning of substantiality,' Babu asserted.

'Babu, you will have to clarify that comment, I don't understand it,' demanded Muniya.

'Certainly, babygirl. What we are absolutely certain of is our own reality, our selfhood. This is so in the interiority of our existence.

'But in the exteriority of experience, what we are absolutely certain of is that we are or have been children, not that we were born, because we don't remember what it was like to be born, nor that we will die, because we don't know what it is like to be dead, nor that we will be happy or miserable tomorrow, because we don't know this either.

'And we cannot dissociate our certainty regarding being children from the memory of our mothers, the companionship of a feminine form, however briefly, without which childhood cannot endure.

'So Yudhishthira's answer that a mother is heavier than the earth can be understood to mean that a girl-child as such, and not only her mother-form, images absolute certainty, the self-certainty of self-awareness, Atman.

'The practice of brahmacharya in Hinduism has as its goal the attainment of self-realisation, the most fully unfurled form of the self-certainty of self-awareness, of which the girl-child is the most luminous portrait imaginable.

'So far from being responsible for the miserable state of the girl-child in India, brahmacharya, rightly understood, would also be a vision of the special spiritual significance of the girl-child, of the condition of womanhood in all its stages of manifestation....

'Not brahmacharya, but our failure to understand its meaning, is responsible for India's (but not only India's) failure to honour the girl-child adequately,' Babu clarified.

'And what were the other two questions which the Yaksha asked Yudhishthira, Babu?' Muniya asked with increasing curiosity.

'What is taller than the sky?' is the second question, and 'What is the most amazing fact of life?' is the third question.

'Yudhishthira's answer to the second question is: "A father is taller than the sky".

'Muniya, here the idea of a father has to be understood as the idea of the source of all manifestation, Atman again, limitless self-awareness which exceeds the farthest reaches of space or sky.

'The notion of Atman is India's chief philosophical resource for dealing with inter-religious conflict, the idea that all human beings, individuals and communities, are self-images of ourselves, indeed all that is, including nothingness, is self's self-image.

'Yudhishthira's answer to the Yaksha's third question: "What is the most amazing fact of life?" is: "The fact that I see people die around me, but I cannot believe that I will die".

'Muniya, the answer is contained in the idea that in seeing people die, as in the terrorist attack on the twin towers of New York last year, I cannot believe that I have died, that self-awareness has perished. I can still see all as myself, self-images of self, the living and the dead, the guilty and the innocent: and be summoned to create a better world, a better self-image of self. This is hard-work, art-work, the medium unwavering self-awareness. To think of the world as other than myself is indeed illusion, Maya, the cause of vengeance and violence, not their cure.

'Muniya, there, in Yudhishthira's answers to the Yaksha's viva questions are the elements of the answers that meet the petulant challenge of your examiners,' Babu concluded, his whispered lecture resulting in a fit of coughing.

The woman in the seat in front of his looked back angrily.

Babu's response this time was not apologetic.

'Dear lady, it was hard to learn English for us in India, but we can't cough silently yet.'

'That's enough, Babu, go to sleep now!' Muniya commanded.

'Let us indeed call it a day now, but I have to tell you that the Yaksha was immensely pleased with Yudhishthira's answers. He was all-upholding Dharma, and had taken the form of a deer and disappeared with the brahmana family's arani sticks to test the Pandavas, representative human beings, to find out if they still had the wisdom to sustain life on the earth.'

'And Babu, Dharma was satisfied that humanity is not lost yet. I will think about that powerful story. Sleep well Babu.'

Terror

It was with great reluctance of spirit that Babu moved his head away from its storytelling proximity to Muniya's form. Resting it and his left shoulder against the wall of the aeroplane, Babu pulled down the window shutter and let Muniya curl up on her seat at an angle away from him. And as the two solicited sleep under light blankets, he sensed a cloud of consciousness carrying them through world after world, life after life, pairing them in myriad ways, separating and uniting them again.

Babu noticed that Muniya's eyes were closed but her mouth moved sidewards testingly, as if she were trying to hear the words of Babu's story in her own voice and subjecting them to a test of truth by 'taste'. Consoled by the sensuous thought, Babu slipped into sleep, and a revelatory nightmare.

Babu sensed that he was formlessly located somewhere in an expanse of the night-sky which surrounded the aircraft, strong moonlight lighting up empty space like a stage. Always troubled by the glare of strong moonlight, Babu heard himself say, 'Put down the shutters, please!'

This was very likely his unconscious plea not to be subjected to the unmasking light of a dream. But the depth of truth, fathomless unconsciousness, dismissed his petition and he found three judges (two of them looked like clerics, the third like a corporate executive: inputs of Muniya's scrolled prints of Francis Bacon?) sitting astride sleek missiles.

And they blew football referee whistles, causing the missiles to belch fire which reduced the Air India Boeing to a large metal sheet suspended in the air, a canvas on which were pinned all the passengers and crew of the aircraft, writhing or dead.

From his invisible location of formlessness, Babu was able to see this graffiti of terror clearly as the smoke of devastation drifted away.

He could see all the figures impaled on the metal canvas, but not Muniya.

And then he saw the three judges astride their missiles and about to blow their whistles again.

Babu pleaded with them for three minutes' to say his last prayers. The judges said nothing, nor did they remove the whistles from their mouths.

'Muniya! Muniya meri, where are you?' Babu shouted.

'Ramana, impale me along with all other passengers, but show me my Muniya! Take her away to safety, Ramana!'

And then Babu saw a cloud drift by near the canvas of disaster. A hand-pulled unoccupied rickshaw (trademark Tyeb Mehta) stood on the cloud. The word 'svaraj' was hand-painted on its back.

'Its operator, Muniya, sweating profusely, was trying to pull out one of the wheels of the rickshaw that had sunk into the cloud, the indubitable reality of self-awareness. The other wheel, self's limitless self-imaging diversity, had also begun to disappear into the depths of delusion.

One of the judges removed the whistle from his mouth and said, 'That's one minute gone, Ms Kulkarni,' and put the whistle back in his mouth.

Babu was besides himself with joy at the sight of Muniya unharmed, although in deadly danger, and chanted. 'Aum Sri

Ramanaya Namah', his mantra of obeisance, with the intensity of concentration with which the child Muniya had looked at him when he had first chanted that mantra in her presence.

And then there emerged on the cloud of judgement a labourer, none other than Ramana, who joined Muniya in extricating the wheels of self-awareness and self-imaging, foundations of svaraj, from invisibility and ignorance.

The wheels were out in no time, and the sage and the girl-child pulled the rickshaw towards the canvas-cross to bring to self-crucifying humanity the resurrecting vehicle of self-realisation.

Babu woke up in sweat on his seat in the aircraft, whispering, 'Muniya, Muniya, are you all right? Where are you?'

Babu opened his eyes to find Muniya looking chidingly at him.

'You dream too much, Babu, Ayi and Baba always said that. You are all right, don't worry about me. I am here, by your side. Go back to sleep.'

In London With Haren Desai

Both Babu and Muniya had managed in the cramped space of aircraft toilets to change into fresh clothes, which they thought would be a gesture of courtesy towards Haren Desai, their host who was going to receive them at the Heathrow airport.

Babu emerged in black corduroy trousers, a grey kurta, a black woollen khadi 'bandi' or 'jawahar jacket', black peshavari chappals, black socks and a long grey scarf. He thought the predominance of black in his attire would be an appropriate gesture of mourning for the victims of the 9/11 catastrophe.

Muniya had asked Babu what she should wear. Babu's close questioning revealed that she had in her canvas bag (in the luggage cabin above their seats) a 'pull on' 'eight-yard-long-looking' martial Maharashtrian sari her Ayi had designed for her. (Babu recalled that a child-version of such a sari had been created by Archana for Muniya out of the white khadi 'thaan' that he had brought as a gift for the Kulkarni children from Tiruvannamalai in 1984.)

Archana had also made out of the same material a short kurta to go with the 'Jhansi-ki-Rani' sari for baby Muniya, with mirror work and dagger motifs, very feminine and 'shakta' at the same time. And Muniya had glowed in that suit on her fourth birthday. Babu described the kurta to Muniya.

'Do you have a similar top?' Babu asked Muniya.

'Babu your appreciation of my fourth birthday suit seems to have made a deep impression on Ayi, because I have an adult version of the same kurta (with mirrors and dagger motifs) to go with the pull-on sari. But the sari and the kurta are both deep rust in colour, and they are handloom not khadi. And I have a dark red American adivasi shawl to go with that ensemble,' Muniya revealed generously, as she could see Babu's face lighting up with joy at her description of this treasure in her canvas bag.

'Wear that suit please, brave Muniya, it will communicate the courage which must never be forsaken by grieving, and correct the one-sidedness of the mainly black clothes I am going to wear,' pleaded Babu.

Soon they were in the Air India section of the airport's baggage-retrieval hall, a study in black, grey, rust and red.

There was no sign of their bags tumbling down the luggage slide. Both sat down on their trolleys, resignedly, their eyes nevertheless compulsively glued to the procession of 'other people's' luggage.

Another 'neti, neti' experience. Babu mentioned to Muniya that that is how he had waited for her to manifest at the airport in San Francisco.

Muniya was encouraged by this parallel to ask Babu to explain in more visual terms (preferably with the aid of the images of great paintings which she may also have encountered during her study of Art and Religion) the idea of the girl-child being a perfect portrait of Atman, of which he had spoken to her on the plane when he told her the Mahabharata story of the missing 'arani sticks' and Yudhishthira's questioning by the Yaksha.

Muniya had worn a black rudraksha mala round her neck, and that immediately reminded Babu of two paintings of Amrita Sher-Gil which he thought profoundly illumined the relationship between the girl-child and Atman, and he asked Muniya if she knew Sher-Gil's work.

'Yes I do, Babu. Vivan Sundaram, Sher-Gil's painter nephew, had been a visiting scholar at Santa Barbara, and he showed us a video of masses of Amrita's work. Why do you ask?'

'Muniya, my meditative Muniya, I hope you have seen a Sher-Gil self-portrait which shows her as a radiant woman wearing an exquisite gold or diamond necklace.

'And I am certain you have seen Amrita's great oil work "Brahmacharis", which shoots like a still photograph a small huddle of young students of the Vedas, very Keralite in appearance, who are not meditating with eyes closed but looking at their viewers with uninhibited curiosity. Some of them would become lifelong sadhakas of self-realisation, others would marry and have children.'

'I recall both works vividly, Babu, what do they say to you?' Muniya asked.

'I wish your viva examiners had asked you questions on art as well, and not only about terrorism and Hinduism's capabilities of dealing with it,' Babu reflected.

'I didn't give them much of a chance, did I, Babu, I walked off!' Muniya replied self-critically.

'They didn't make it easy for you to sit for long, did they?' Babu retorted.

'We'll talk about all that later, Babu, you are not concentrating. Back to Sher-Gil!' decreed Muniya.

'Muniya, imagine the two paintings facing each other, so we can think of Amrita, a gloriously unfurled and adorned girl-child, like you, looking at the young brahmacharis and they at her.

'She would in the interiority of self-consciousness be absolutely certain of her reality: "I am".

'The explosion of that certainty of self-awareness into the all-pervasive light of self-realisation, moksha, would be the goal of of the brahmacharis' sadhana.

'But in the exteriority of their experience of a world of apparent otherness surrounding them, they would be scrutinising every encountered form in the hope of finding a portrait, a symbolic likeness, of Atman.

'Muniya, I put it to you that in Amrita's "self-portrait" the boys find just that, a self-portrait (portrait of self, Atman!). Their remembered childhood blossomed in the form of their unforgettable mothers as a radiantly beautiful feminine form.

'An "ardhanarishvara" realisation, the other half here being childhood's indubitable reality.

'And for Amrita, the childhood of the brahmachari boys would symbolise the unfading freshness of self-awareness.

'Beauty and beatitude mirroring one another ...,' Babu could have gone on and on, but vigilant Muniya spotted her bags and lifted them off the rolling slide in great style, her rust armour and swinging rudraksha bringing to her act of retrieval a quality of heroic beauty which a group of Franciscan monks standing nearby beheld with awe.

Babu too retrieved his luggage, less athletically than Muniya, but unaided. With their loaded trolleys, and nothing to declare, Babu and Muniya were able to sail through customs and soon found themselves in the 'waiting' area at Heathrow teeming with subcontinental humanity.

A tall black youth dressed informally in denims and with a clean-shaven head came running towards them and asked them if they were Professor Ravi Srivastava and Ms Ananya Kulkarni.

'That's right,' said Babu, and the youth revealed that he, George, Nigerian student and a former Iskcon devotee, had been instructed by Mr Desai, who was waiting to receive them outside the reception area, to find them and bring them safely and quickly to the vehicle (a Rolls Royce, as it turned out) in which he would drive them to the Desai home off Russell Square.

'Krishna was a charioteer, wasn't he?' said Muniya, and this pleased the Nigerian immensely.

Amrita Sher-Gil, 1934; Detail from Brahmacharis, Amrita Sher-Gil, 1937

'I love Krishna, but I don't much like organised religion of any kind,' George confessed.

'That makes three of us!' Babu declared, and all laughed.

They found Haren Desai standing next to a shining black Rolls Royce, glued to a cell phone.

'Yes, yes, Dr Patwardhan, Professor Srivastava has just arrived,' Desai said to a caller and waved a greeting to Babu and Muniya.

'No, he can't talk to you just now. Yes, you can distribute your questions to the audience before the lecture. No, he can't address a Hyde Park assembly!'

Formal greetings and introductions followed.

Desai explained that he was being constantly called by Dr Shrinivas Patwardhan, a veteran Indian freedom fighter who had read Babu work, *The Testimony of Janaka*, and disagreed violently with it, and wanted to engage Babu in a series of debates on the issues raised in that book.

However, as the sponsor of Babu's (three hours long) lecture at the Bharatiya Vidya Bhavan on the theme 'Hinduism and Violence', he, Haren Desai, was not going to impose extra responsibilities on Professor Srivastava.

Babu and Desai sat in the back seat of the Rolls Royce. Democratic Muniya was happy to sit in the passenger seat in the front next to George.

Haren Desai revealed that he had been evicted from Uganda by Idi Amin many years ago. But by the grace of their family deity, Sri Krishna, his diamond business had flourished. He had started work in London as a grocer in the backyard of Russell Square, but had worked round the clock and saved and invested wisely and was now the owner of a five-bedroom apartment in a building not far from the grocery store he had started.

'My wife Gangaben, my son Gautam (he helps me in my business which reaches out to all corners of the world) and daughter-in-law Pushpa (who is studying social anthropology at the London School of Economics) are all looking forward to meeting you, Professor Srivastava, and your friend's daughter Ananya.

'A light Gujarati dinner awaits us. You will have separate bedrooms, and if, before the lecture which has been fixed for tomorrow evening, you would like to travel around in London, George will be your chauffeur and my humble Rolls your vehicle.'

'Babu, there is a retrospective exhibition of Francis Bacon at the Tate Gallery starting tomorrow. I couldn't possibly miss it!' Muniya announced through the open glass curtain between the front and rear portions of the car.

'I would love to see the Bacon show with you, Muniya. Without confronting the brutal honesty of Bacon's perception of a human being as nothing more than a decaying body and a despairing mind, Advaita Vedanta cannot be understood with any measure of un-self-deceivingness,' Babu replied, and thanked his host profusely for inviting him to London.

'May I come with you to the Bacon exhibition?' George asked Babu and also looked at Muniya for her reaction to his request.

'We'd love you to!' said Babu and Muniya simultaneously.

Haren Desai's cell phone rang again.

'George, I am not taking that call, it must be Dr Patwardhan again. Let's go home. I am sure our guests are hungry!' commanded Desai, and switched off his mobile.

Muniya suddenly turned around and looked at Babu, empowering him with her trademark smile.

Out of the traffic around the airport, the Rolls ran along the motorway, homeward bound, like an unstoppable 'ashvamedha' horse.

Sinking into his seat, arms folded across his ample waist, eyes closed, Harenbhai initiated a long conversation.

'Ravi Saheb, if you don't mind my so addressing you, may I request you to tell us a story from the Ramayana or the Mahabharata which addresses the question of the travails of the human body, its deep dissatisfaction even with its hard-won pleasures.

'I have not seen Francis Bacon's works, although I am sure my daughter-in-law Pushpa has. My business leaves me with little time to visit galleries, but I am aware that Bacon evokes the enormity of the anguish of bodily existence. I would be grateful, Ravi Saheb, if you could help me gain some pauranika understanding of the terribly mixed blessings of biology.'

'And me, said George.'

'Me too, Babu!' pleaded Muniya, turning her head back towards Babu with a "Do well!" frown. In the process, she managed to throw her pigtail over her seat into the rear cabin of the vehicle, whose knotted end Babu caught between his hands like a cricket ball at first slip, his favourite fielding position.

'Aum Sri Ramanaya Namah,' Babu chanted gratefully, and readily responded to Harenbhai's request.

'Harenbhai, there is a Ramayana story which addresses the question of bodily life and its continuity directly, and I will recall it for all of you presently.

'But I am tempted first to bless my squirrel-quick Muniya by running my thumb down her pigtail, as Sri Rama blessed a squirrel who was the most inspired member of the work-gang of all life which was engaged in building a bridge between the continent of Bharata, all-comprehensive Atman, and "Lanka", which literally means ego, exclusivity.

'Because even ego is self's own distorted form and cannot fall outside its sphere of compassion.'

As Harenbhai looked on puzzled, Babu ran his thumb down Muniya's head all the way to the bottom of her pigtail, rolling it up and letting it roll down again in her cabin, accompanying this act with the chant 'tat tvam asi'.

'May the blessing of Sri Rama's self-symbolising thumb be with you always, my gilehri!' Babu said.

George, whose head was clean-shaven, a link with his erstwhile Iskcon connection he did not want to snap, felt terribly upset at this point, and asked Babu in lamenting tones if his bald head disqualified him from Sri Rama's Atman-blessing!

'Of course not, George, your head receives the ceaseless blessings of the sky, which is Atman's own Buddha-form of all-inclusive emptiness!' Babu responded with humorous immediacy, causing Muniya and George to clap and Harenbhai to scream, 'Back to the steering-wheel, George!'

'Sorry, Mr Desai, but I was provoked by happiness into that momentary act of surrender to the divine,' George said, with a hint of sarcasm which Harenbhai didn't comprehend, but Muniya did, causing her to giggle with her hand covering her mouth, a very Indian gesture to which Harenbhai's beloved daughter-in-law, Pushpa, often resorted. Harenbhai forgave George and urged Babu to begin the Ramayana story he had promised to narrate.

'Dear Harenbhai, George, and beloved Muniya, listen, listen to this sacred story from the Ramayana.

'Even before he became a Brahmarshi, a self-realised sage, King Vishvamitra's heroic austerities had brought to him many siddhis, occult powers, and he was much admired by the high and mighty of the land, and sought after especially because Vishvamitra was susceptible to flattery and this enabled them to receive many boons from him.' Those were the 'introductory' words with which Babu commenced his story.

'Babu, you don't start your stories badly at all, you know! Muniya said mock-flatteringly and also to test how free of ego Babu was.

'Naughty gilehri, don't think I am flattered by those words of yours at all! But you can ask for any boon you want, I'll pass your request on to Ramana!' Babu said defensively.

Muniya laughed and said she was only teasing him, but Babu knew in his heart that Muniya had commenced an internal viva-voce examination of his progress towards egolessness.

Babu returned to the story with a greater sense of responsibility towards its sacred content. ('Won't you always be my conscience, babygirl?' he asked her telepathically. She rolled her pigtail back into the rear cabin compassionately, but before Babu could be distracted by it, pulled it back!)

'Hard taskmaster!' muttered Babu in his heart, and was now in full flow.

'A King, Trishanku was his name, which suggests that he was, metaphorically, "not" "on all fours", approached Vishvamitra and proclaimed that there was no greater sage than Vishvamitra in the land and that is why he, Trishanku, had sought him out, and begged to be forgiven his intrusiveness.

'Flattered, Vishvamitra forgave Trishanku's intrusiveness immediately, and asked what the King wanted.

'Now Trishanku had contracted leprosy and his family and subjects had driven him out of his home and kingdom. So great was Trishanku's love of embodied life, though, that he didn't want to die but be bodily transported to heaven.

'Great Sage, fulfil this wish of mine. I will proclaim your greatness in all three worlds!

'Ignoring the warnings of other sages, Vishvamitra meditated on Shiva with all his spiritual energy and asked him to let Trishanku rise to heaven there and then, in that leprosy-stricken body of his.

'Trishanku rose into the sky and reached heaven's gate, but the gatekeepers were appalled by the King's appearance and cast him down and he started falling back towards the earth, screaming wildly: "Vishvamitra, save me!"

'Vishvamitra, undeterred, prayed to Shiva again and asked Trishanku to be stationed in mid-heaven. Shiva obliged and Vishvamitra poured all his remaining spiritual energy into creating an alternative "technological" universe around Trishanku.

'At this point all the gods approached Vishvamitra and urged him to stop right there, and not disrupt the coherence of the universe and fuel the ambition of egoistic physicality, as this was likely to undermine the saving sadhana of self-realisation in which all life was engaged, knowingly or unknowingly: the realisation of self's singularity and the limitless diversity of its self-imaging.

'Harenbhai, George, Muniya! This is the sadhana which seeks an end to the delusion that we are nothing but our bodily forms, the delusion which causes Francis Bacon's figures to scream in agony.

'The sadhana of self-realisation also seeks to end the delusion that we are not our bodily forms at all, but a non-material "soul" whose proper place is heaven. This is also what makes Bacon's Pope figures scream in agony.

'Because if we are only our bodily forms, and these must one day perish, we may want to advance that hour of dissolution, encouraging collective human suicide!

'And if we are not our bodily forms at all, but a non-physical soul whose residence is heaven, we might want to advance the hour of our arrival in heaven, allowing all life on earth to perish in the process, if necessary!

'And the homosexual coupling of many of Bacon's figures may have a deeper meaning than partisan views on the subject would suggest.

'Given the annihilationism built into the "trishanku", unbalanced, view of ourselves, the likely non-reproductivity of our species cannot be more powerfully portrayed than by the symbolism of homosexual coupling.'

George and Muniya caught each other's eye in amazement at this unorthodox reading of the joyless sexual engagement of Bacon's male figures.

Harenbhai stared in disbelief at the relevance of pauranika wisdom to contemporary dilemmas of non-conformity.

George had driven through Kew Gardens, Hammersmith, Kensington, and other suburbs, with unflagging concentration, and with close attention to the Trishanku story. (Hyde Park, Marble Arch, Soho, the British Museum, all passed by without a comment from him for the benefit of the visitors). And when the story ended, they were home, the towering building off Russell Square on the fifth floor of which was the Desai apartment.

The light Gujarati meal promised by Harenbhai turned out to be a feast of vegetarian Gujarati cuisine: super-thin rotis, sweetened osaman dal, several varieties of vegetables, fragrant rice, dhoklas, thepla, chhunda, puran poli (common to Gujarat and Maharashtra, Muniya polished off a couple of them, to Gangaben's great delight), and, inevitably, shrikhand for dessert.

Gautam and Pushpa, Harenbhai's son and daughter-in-law, were dazzled by Muniya's martial attire in rust handloom, and she promised to mail them its design and stitching secrets after extacting them from her mother.

At the end of the meal, Muniya offered to help Pushpa with washing-up chores. Gangaben would hear nothing of it, but Babu explained to her that she should let Muniya experience the pleasure of sharing this responsibility with Pushpa, because Sri Krishna had himself cleared all the leaf-plates after Yudhishthira's Rajasuya Yajna feast. Not only because no task was too, unimportant to be done by him with the perfection of detachment, but also to symbolise that when we have enjoyed the feast of life, our bodies, like leaf plates, are taken away by God himself, the ultimate scavenger, servant, and recycled into new life.

Before retiring to their separate bedrooms for the night, Babu and Muniya expressed a desire to view the special Francis Bacon show at the Tate Gallery in the morning.

'We'll be back around lunch time. But Gangaben, I will only eat some khicchri, otherwise I'll go to sleep during the lecture in the evening. I don't speak for Muniya, of course,' Babu quickly qualified.

'I am only going to eat fruit tomorrow, Babu, a partial observance of Ekadashi which is a day of complete fasting for Ayi,' was Muniya's austerity-matching response.

Harenbhai called George on his cell phone and asked him to take Professor Srivastava and Ms Ananya Kulkarni to the Tate Gallery at ten in the morning, and not fail, repeat, not fail, to bring them back home by 1 p.m.

Considerate Muniya requested Gangaben to replace the foam mattress in Babu's bedroom with a cotton mattress, there was no special advantage to be gained by his lecturing with accentuated rheumatism.

'Sleep well, because you must do well tomorrow!' that was her 'goodnight' command to Babu, softened by a lightning smile.

Babu woke up in the middle of the night, terrorised by a second run of his aeroplane nightmare.

He stepped out of his bedroom softly and sat down at the dining table with a glass of water.

'Muniya, where are you?' he moaned, as softly as he could, so as not to disturb anyone.

Muniya, alert gilehri, and no one else, heard Babu, and she came and sat down next to him.

Babu recalled all the details of his aeroplane dream, and begged her to summon him whenever the wheels of her life needed to be pulled out of the mire of unhappiness or the clouds of delusion.

'Yes I will Babu, tatumsi, tatumsi, goodnight!' said Muniya.

Francis Bacon's Intervention

The Desai chariot was transporting Babu and Muniya to the riverside site of the Tate Gallery. George at the wheel of the Rolls Royce seemed to be in a genial mood, humming the Beatles' 'Indian' number – 'Within you and without you'.

Babu would have loved to participate in some intercultural, intergenerational conversation on the theme and amiable musicality of the song, perhaps even to suggest a brief stopover at Trafalgar Square and urge Muniya to feed the pigeons around Nelson's column, but he was troubled by her unmoved rock-profile, not turning back even once to smile or talk to him, or even sideways to exchange words of ritual goodwill with George.

'Is she angry with me for waking her up last night and sharing the terrifying details of my nightmare with her?' Babu wondered. And fell into prayer and sleep.

Unbeknownst to Babu, that is when Muniya turned around and suffered what can only be called a hallucination.

Babu was wearing a black woollen pullover over his black corduroys.

Muniya saw a suddenly aged Babu, the hair on his head bone-white and grossly depleted, the flesh around his neck hanging in multiple folds, his mouth dribbling with saliva all over the high neck of his pullover, his fingers trembling, possibly Parkinsonian, hands failing to knit into one another in prayer. Crotch soaked in urine.

'George! Pull up by the pavement for a minute, I think Babu is dead or dying!' Muniya shouted.

'Babu was fast asleep and could hear nothing.

George brought the Rolls Royce to a full stop in three seconds flat by the riverside pavement.

The jolt woke Babu up.

And it released Muniya from her hallucination.

She saw that Babu's hair was more grey than black, yes, the flesh on his face was not firm like her's or George's, but he was not dribbling saliva on to his pullover collar, and the fingers of his hands were untremblingly knitted into one another in a gesture of devotion. His trousers unembarrassingly dry.

'Muniya, sorry I dozed off. I didn't sleep too well last night. Is everything all right? Have we been in an accident? Are we near the Tate?' Babu asked apologetically.

For an entire minute Muniya and George stared at Babu, and then at one another, and Muniya started to cry.

George, sensing that he might be invading privacy, stepped out of the vehicle and stood against the low wall overlooking the fast-flowing river.

'Muniya meri, don't cry. I was distressed to find you looking so withdrawn in the car even several minutes after we started off from Russell Square this morning. My midnight ramblings must have upset you. I am sorry. But don't cry my babygirl. I adore your silences, your rock-still face is a siddhi sought without success by the best of yogins. But don't cry! Tell me what has troubled you?' Babu pleaded like a child.

Muniya described her hallucination of Babu's physical degeneration, and confessed her fear that Babu and the whole tradition of Advaita Vedanta might be deluded, that Francis

Bacon's vision might be the bitter truth of our being, despite all the illuminating stories and explanations with which Babu had sought to instruct and entertain her since they started their strange new journey in San Francisco a few days earlier.

'Babu, I am not a philosopher, although I would like to learn philosophy, especially Indian philosophy, from you.

'But I fear that you don't want to believe that we are but this decaying body and despairing mind because you care for me deeply and want to protect me from harsh reality!

'Convince me, Babu, that my hunch about the biased basis of your advaitin conviction is wrong!'

Babu suggested to Muniya that they too might benefit from some fresh air and the sight of the flowing Thames, and were soon standing beside it.

'Muniya I do indeed care for you deeply and would like to protect you from all unhappiness, but not from truth, because untruth cannot sustain happiness.

'Tell me my gudiya, why does anything flow? Like that river, like the breeze which is blowing your hair all over my face. Why does one breath follow another?

'Because nothing is only where it appears to be, but everywhere. We are also not located only in youth and well-being, or only in old age and suffering and death, but in all conditions of life.

'And in nothingness too, not in things, merely.

'Our eyes are glad to be able in an instant to make contact with the infinitely distant sky, which is also in our hands, close to us.

'We are everywhere, in all things, we "are" all things, that is why we are able to love what is far and what is at hand.

'Muniya, the testimony of our eyes and our hearts goes against the one-sided conclusion that we are nothing but this bodily form.

'Francis Bacon's despairing vision is unfair not only to the idea of Atman or self, but to the reality of our physicality too.

'An upanishadic sage has the last word on this subject.

'I am indeed this old man bent upon a stick, he says. Yes, Muniya, I, Babu, am also the frightening vision of decay you saw.

'But the sage goes on to say, "I am also that pretty girl standing over there".

'Muniya pyari, I am also you.

'The sage doesn't stop here. He goes on to say, "I am also that green bird with red eyes".

'Ecological prophet, that sage. "Green bird with red eyes", unbeatable metaphor of provoked nature.

'Muniya, we are all things and nothingness too.

'In saying this I celebrate your inclusiveness, which includes and transmutes unhappiness into compassion. I do not hide unhappiness from you.'

Babu could have gone on and on, but Muniya interrupted him.

'Your lecture is in the evening, Babu, at the Bharatiya Vidya Bhavan, not at the Tate Gallery.

'Let's look at Bacon's pictures. At their brutal honesty, to use your phrase. The inevitability of exclusivism's scream!' Muniya exclaimed solemnly, and laughed.

George and Muniya and Babu exposed themselves for a long time to the power of Bacon's works: the disfiguring imprisonment of self in the prison of exclusivist identity, secular or religious, the non-replicability of self-distorted life.

George deposited Babu and Muniya in the lift of the Desai apartment building in time for lunch.

On their way up, Babu asked Muniya to look at herself in the mirror, and she did so with her signature smile.

'Muniya, your sideward-moving mouth is a reminder of the redundancy of speech in the face of the testimony of your widening, inclusive eyes.'

'Yes, Babu, but your lecture is not redundant. Stop dreaming, start moving! This is the fifth floor.'

'Hinduism and Violence': A Lecture At The Bharatiya Vidya Bhavan

Two vehicles took the Desais and their guests to the Bharatiya Vidya Bhavan, the West Kensington venue for Ravi Srivastava's lecture on 'Hinduism and Violence', scheduled to start at 6 p.m.

Gautam and his mother Gangaben and wife Pushpa had reached the venue independently in Gautam's Mercedes at 5.30 p.m. to make sure that all arrangements for the lecture were in place.

With Harenbhai and Babu in the back cabin, a grinning Muniya in the front passenger seat ('Hi George!' she said with genuine warmth, atoning for her apparent rudeness earlier during the day), George drove the Rolls skilfully down London's less traffic-ridden lanes and manifested it under the Bhavan's main porch precisely at 5.45 p.m., the time of arrival for the evening's lecturer suggested to Harenbhai by the Bhavan's secretary, N. Subramaniam, who greeted the party with a single but enduring gesture of folded hands, namaste, and led them to his office.

Subramaniam was going to chair the evening's programme sponsored by Haren Desai (who was dressed in a white silk 'bandgala' suit. Babu hadn't abandoned the black corduroys and black jersey he had worn for the visit to the Tate, he wanted to 'look the same, such as he was' to Muniya).

George parked his vehicle in the Bhavan's parking lot near Gautam's Mercedes. He had been personally invited by Babu to attend the lecture and found a good seat in the rear for himself.

The auditorium was filling up.

Muniya detached herself from the ritual observances of hospitality in Subramaniam's office and sat down next to Pushpa in the third row from the podium. A large framed photograph of Sri Ramakrishna Paramahamsa in sankeertana dance hung on the wall above the podium, with a slight tilt.

Sankeertana lover, George, ran down the length of the auditorium and up the podium and corrected the tilt, risking his job, but triggered appreciative clapping from Muniya and the entire audience. Catcalls indicated the mixed class-character of the assembly, and this delighted gilehri Muniya.

The celebratory noise brought N. Subramaniam and Haren Desai and Ravi Srivastava on to the podium in a hurry. Subramaniam took the middle chair, Harenbhai sat in the chair to his left, Babu in a similar chair to his right.

Muniya's off-white khadi silk sari and blouse, jet-black hair and large brown forehead heightened the radiance of her Modigliani face.

Subramaniam was smiling at Muniya, unable to take his eyes off her. Babu hadn't noticed her yet.

Gangaben sat next to Pushpa on the other side and Gautam next to her, all elegantly dressed.

The clock on the wall opposite the podium struck six and Subramaniam rose from his chair with a clutch of notes in his left hand, and walked up to the lectern near Babu's chair. He was about to begin the evening's proceedings, when an elegant old man dressed in a three-piece suit and a hat entered the auditorium with shuffling feet and shouted a protest:

'Mr Subramaniam, I, Dr Shrinivas Patwardhan, a veteran freedom fighter, had personally delivered to your office five hundred copies of a note listing my objections to Professor

Srivastava's book *The Testimony of Janaka*, with a request that they be distributed to the audience before the lecture. Why has this not been done? Mr Haren Desai had not objected to my request. Why have you disregarded it?'

George helped Dr Shrinivas Patwardhan find a chair, but he preferred to remain standing, wagging his forefinger and demanding an explanation from Subramaniam for what he took to be an act of grave discourtesy to his person.

Babu got up and greeted Dr Patwardhan with a namaste and assured him that some of his questions (Babu had read the note listing them in Subramaniam's office) would be dealt with by him during the lecture and the discussion that would follow.

Dr Patwardhan sat down reluctantly and a greatly relieved Subramaniam began his introductory speech.

'Shri Haren Desai, Professor Ravi Srivastava, dear friends:

'Welcome to the Bharatiya Vidya Bhavan.

'My special thanks to Shri Haren Desai for making it possible for the Bhavan to host this evening's lecture by Professor Ravi Srivastava on the theme "Hinduism and Violence", as part of our "Contemporary Indian Spirituality" project of lectures and discussions.

'Professor Ravi Srivastava was born in Allahabad in 1944 and studied philosophy both in India, at Delhi University, where he also briefly flowered as a leg break-googly bowler, and in Britain, at the University of Aberdeen in Scotland, where he played no cricket at all.

'On returning to India in 1971, Ravi Srivastava taught philosophy for four years at Hindu College in Delhi, where he had studied philosophy for a BA (honours) degree.

'Following a period of disillusionment with modern western philosophy because of its neglect of the notion of self, and its tragic reduction of the reality of self-consciousness to the fiction of a supposed consciousness which can only be conscious of something other than itself, never of itself, a reduction to which Professor Srivastava traces the propensity of modern civilisation to unredeemable violence, Srivastava lived for several years in

Tiruvannamalai, the sacred town in Tamil Nadu where Sri Ramana Maharshi had lived and taught the truth of self-realisation for more than half a century.

'In Tiruvannamalai, Ravi Srivastava studied the life and teachings of Ramana Maharshi and also engaged in the sadhana of self-realisation as taught by Ramana, but which he says has not yet consummated in moksha!'

'Not at all! exclaimed Babu,' and that is when he noticed Muniya in the front rows. Her eyes were closed. 'You are doing well, Babu, even if you are acting. But do better!' was her psychic command which Babu sensed more tangibly than the pain in his rheumatic lower back.

'Be that as it may,' Subramaniam continued, 'Ravi Srivastava wrote a number of articles in philosophical journals in India and abroad on the teachings of Sri Ramana Maharshi and its relevance to our times. For a year, in 1981, he was Professor of Comparative Religion at Shantiniketan, the university founded by the great poet and savant Rabindranath Tagore.

'After a period of study and pilgrimage in Pune in 1984, during which he became greatly drawn to the life and teachings of Sri Jnaneshvara Maharaj, Srivastava spent several years in Dakshineshvara, Pondicherry, Delhi, Sevagram and Sabarmati, studying the lives and teachings of Sri Ramakrishna Paramahamsa, Svami Vivekananda, Sri Aurobindo and Mahatma Gandhi.

'Pune University published many of his essays on these teachers as a book entitled *Five Sages*. A brief stint as Professor of Philosophy at the University of Hyderabad followed the publication of that work.

'In 1991, following the political and spiritual turmoil into which India was thrown by the Ayodhya agitation, Srivastava wrote a book entitled *The Testimony of Janaka*, in which he attempted to restore to Sita a position of spiritual and philosophical importance which traditions of Ramayana scholarship have by and large neglected, an injustice to which Srivastava traces the propensity of Indian, and not merely Hindu, society, to treat the female child with cruelty throughout all stages of her life.

'The book has attracted much attention, as was evident by Dr Shrinivas Patwardhan's interjection at the very beginning of this evening's programme.'

Shrinivas Patwardhan was on his feet again, ready to elaborate his objections to Professor Srivastava's work on Sita, but Chairman Subramaniam very sternly asked him to be patient. Patwardhan staged a noisy walkout but good old George brought him back to his seat with encouraging words about the possibility of a fruitful dialogue between Ravi and him at an appropriate time which would benefit all.

'Following worldwide condemnation of the nuclear tests conducted by India and Pakistan in 1998, Ravi Srivastava wrote a tract entitled *The Third Atom Bomb*, in which he severely castigated the British Empire for splitting the spiritual unity of Indian civilisation by partitioning India, which resulted in the brutal massacre of nearly two million innocent human beings, and which he likened to the dropping of a third nuclear bomb on human beings after Hiroshima and Nagasaki.

'*The Third Atom Bomb* has not yet been published, although copies of the tract have been widely distributed across the world.

'The California Institute of Integral Studies in San Francisco invited Professor Srivastava to teach courses on the sages of modern India during 1999 and 2000. And again, last month.

'Professor Ravi Srivastava, may I request you now to deliver your lecture?'

Babu walked up to the lectern with his file of notes and a copy of *Talks with Ramana Maharshi*, closed his eyes, folded his hands in namaskara to the audience, and began his lecture.

'You have done me an honour which I am not worthy of, Harenbhai and Subramaniamji, in asking me to deliver a lecture on the theme "Hinduism and Violence" at the Bharatiya Vidya Bhavan in London before this awesome assembly of concerned world citizens: young and old, men and women, believers and sceptics too, I am sure, who are united by a shared interest in the wisdom of Hinduism, and anxiety about the fate of life and civilisation on earth, in the face of growing and worldwide inter-religious and inter-civilisational violence.

'Mr Chairman, I lay my head at the feet of Sadguru Ramana.

'I want you to look at the great picture of Sri Ramakrishna on the wall behind me,' Babu said, turning round himself to look at the dancing form of the sage of Dakshineshvara.

There was sudden loud laughter from the audience, which neither Babu nor Subramaniam nor Desai could comprehend, and they looked at one another and shrugged in amazement.

A tall young woman in a white sari stood up, shook her head vigorously to deny that there was any mischievous basis to the laughter, thereby causing her jooda to unfold and her hair to roll down like a snake, and explained that before the proceedings of the evening began, a young man, who was sitting shyly at the back of the hall, had noticed that the Ramakrishna picture was not hanging straight, but tilting slightly. The young man had straightened the picture and thereby drawn everyone's attention to it. She said it was an astounding coincidence that Professor Srivastava should begin his lecture with a reference to that picture, and that that is what had evoked spontaneous, and happy, laughter from the audience.

'Thank you, bless you!' Babu said to her, without addressing her as Muniya or Ananya, because she had spoken for all, not for herself alone. Non-dualistically, non-violently. Courageously.

'Arun and Archana's daughter, absolutely, my Muniya!' Babu said to himself.

Babu could see the diamond on Muniya's nose and suddenly recalled that the nose of the sculptural form of Goddess Kanyakumari in the temple at Cape Comorin was adorned by a diamond. His attention wavered. Noticing this, Muniya coughed and Babu quickly returned to his lecture.

The Wisdom Of Hissing

'Friends, listen to a Ramakrishna story with attention and devotion. It goes to the heart of the theme of violence and non-violence, and reveals Hinduism's non-dualist unravelling of the malaise of violence and its cure.

'Ramakrishna tells us of a village called Haripur, which was surrounded by an untended field in which there lived a dangerous cobra who bit and killed everyone who dared to cross the field to go to other villages.

'The isolated villagers were devastated. They could not undertake journeys to find grooms for their daughters, nor markets for their produce.

'A sadhu who lived in Banaras heard of their plight from one of the villagers who had taken a long and circuitous route out of the terrorised hamlet to seek divine intervention.

'The sadhu decided at once to walk straight through the dangerous field to Haripur, asking the supplicant to return home by the circuitous route and let the residents of Haripur know of his forthcoming visit.

'Ramakrishna tells us, dear friends, that the sadhu entered the field chanting the name of Hari, fearlessly, and with boundless love for all that is.

'"Hari, Hari, Hari ...," he chanted, and then, near some bushes, he found himself confronted by the cobra who had uncoiled himself and raised his hood high to sting the sadhu on his forehead.

'"My dear brother," said the sadhu with tears in his eyes. "How horribly you must have been treated by misguided people to make you so suspicious and hostile towards everyone. I have been longing for a darshana of the symbol of divine shakti that you are, my obeisance to you!" the sadhu declared.

'The cobra had never heard such words of understanding and respect before and became a disciple of the sadhu, who persuaded him to chant the name of Hari always and not bite anyone at all.

'"I'll come back in a year's time to assess your progress in sadhana!" the sadhu said and walked through the field to Haripur with the good news that the dreaded snake had become a devotee of Hari and would not bite travellers any more.

'After a few weeks the sadhu went away to other villages.

'And the residents of Haripur were surprised to find that they were able to cross the fearful field connecting their village to other villages without the cobra attacking them.

'They found him chanting "Hari, Hari, Hari ...," and even dancing in celebration of the unity of life.

'But urchins soon started taking advantage of the cobra's new-found non-violence and devotion and pelted him with stones every day. The cobra didn't retaliate. Faithful to his Guru's instruction, he kept chanting "Hari, Hari, Hari ...," Soon he was reduced to a mere stretch of skin, barely alive, but still chanting the sacred mantra he had been taught.

'A year later the sadhu returned from his wanderings to the field where he had initiated the cobra into the "Hari" mantra and non-violence.

'He found his disciple hiding in a thorn-bush, without aura or flesh, muttering "Hari, Hari, Hari ...," in a barely audible voice.

'"What have you done to yourself, my dear friend?" the sadhu asked the snake.

'"I have only followed your instruction to chant the name of Hari and not bite anyone. Village urchins beat me every day but I don't bite them," the cobra replied feebly but respectfully.

'"My poor, poor, friend. I am glad you have not ceased to chant the name of Hari. Your sadhana of chanting will bring you illumination in the fullness of time."

'"But I had only asked you not to bite. I didn't ask you not to hiss!" the sadhu said, and restoring the cobra to a more realistic path of sadhana and self-defence, the holy man went away.

'Dear friends, that is the substance of the Ramakrishna story. We can read in it, and so we should, the teaching that the threat of defensive violence is not unethical or unspiritual in this world of cruelty and exploitation of the weak and the meek.

'But if that is all that we read in the story, we would miss the profounder heart of the teaching.

'More seriously the story draws attention to the limitation of our exclusivist identities, the idea that we are only a given bodily form or a given collectivity of bodily forms, for instance.

'Hissing would be a mode of addressing, not targeting, one another. A reminder that we are self-imaged in all forms, including but not exclusively in our own given forms, human or non-human, and therefore, as being inherently capable of "living and letting" live, and not in need of being "coerced" by some code external to our reality to do so.

'The illumination of hissing would discourage us from thinking that we were some non-material "soul" whose proper home is heaven and thus prevented from destroying all life "here" to get quickly to our heavenly home "there"!

'Or, from advancing the hour of the inevitable dissolution of our own physical forms, because the nothingness into which we would suicidally wish to disappear is already a self-image of ours.

'Hissing in this life-respecting way could well be called the mantra of non-dualist non-violence: the proclamation that unavoidable, minimal, violence, is, in its self-restraint, a lucid image of self-sufficient selfhood, svaraj, which alone can sustain the adventure of life and civilisation on earth indefinitely.'

With these words Babu concluded the Ramakrishna story.

The auditorium reverberated with the sound 'Hissss!' which emanated from a corner occupied by rough-looking young men and women, white, brown and black.

Subramaniam decreed a tea break of fifteen minutes.

Was Gandhi A Fraud?

Babu requested a quiet, contemplative, tea break for himself, without any interaction with the audience, and Subramaniam considerately arranged for a cup of tea and some biscuits to be brought to the podium table for him. A similar favour was extended, at Babu's insistence, to elderly Dr Patwardhan, who kept staring at Babu with scorn, but did not hurl anything at him.

The audience formed disciplined and fast-moving queues in the veranda outside the auditorium for refreshments, George urging the Bhavan caterers gently but firmly into rendering quicker service.

Everyone returned to their seats at 7.30 p.m. Subramaniam informed Babu that he could speak for an additional hour. Followed by a discussion for half an hour, the programme could end, as announced, at 9 p.m.

'Welcome back, dear friends.

'The "hiss" mantra taught by Ramakrishna's sadhu bears a remarkable similarity of meaning to the "da" mantra given by Prajapati to the assembly of gods, demons, and humans, his creation, in the well-known upanishadic story.

'Disillusioned with their lot, a group of gods, demons, and humans ventured together in occult prayer to solicit the help of their maker, Prajapati. Encountering him deep in their hearts, they sought a word of illumination from him which would make the life of the gods more meaningful, the life of the demons more secure, and the life of humans more peaceful.

'Prajapati heard their prayer with compassion and uttered the "da" mantra and vanished from the consciousness of the petitioners, leaving them utterly confused.

'The gods meditated earnestly on the mantric sound "da" and, by Prajapati's grace, it dawned on them that "da" was intended by Prajapati to remind them of the importance of "damyata", self-restraint.

'"We must be less greedy, if we want our lives to be more meaningful," they concluded.

'Isn't that a wise prescription for the rich, dear friends?

'To want more and more is to understand less and less the meaning of what we cannot have more of, our being, ourselves. And in tragic forgetfulness of our uncheatable, inner, wealth, to become vulnerable to suicidal and murderous anger at life for refusing to give us all that we want.

'But we must delve deeper into the "da" mantra for the gods, if we want to gain an insight into Hinduism's understanding of the roots of violence.

'Ironically, self-restraint becomes an unstrenuously realisable lifestyle only when we stop thinking of selfhood as our exclusive experience, celebrating the being and well-being of apparent "others" as our own, because apparent others are only variant forms of ourselves.

'Austerity, thus understood, ceases to look like a form of violence against ourselves.

'The demons, too, meditated earnestly on Prajapati's "da" mantra, and by his grace they understood that the sound was intended by him to evoke in them the quality of "daya", mercy, without which they would never be free from the fear that those whom they oppress would wreak vengeful violence upon them.

Mahatma Gandhi, Noakhali, 1947

'Friends, isn't that a wise realisation for the powerful, the punitive, and the oppressive in all worlds?

'But we must reflect more on the "da" instruction for the demons if we wish to gain deeper insight into Hinduism's understanding of violence and its cure.

'Mercy most profoundly demands to be exercised upon oneself, on one's idea of who or what one is.

'If we don't see that our manifest forms are also a self-image of self, that we are not some other "more real and enduring" form of manifestation or non-manifestation, as opposed to our present form, we are likely to remain vulnerable to the temptation to destroy everything in the given order of manifestation and be restored to our "true" condition.

'Humans also unearthed a meaning and message in the sacred sound "da" which addressed their condition uniquely.

'"Da" is "datta", an appeal to us to give, share, not be possessive, selfish, they reflected.

'How can there be peace on earth if we don't share what we have with all human beings?

'Friends, without an agenda of justice, can there be any prospects for peace?

'But the Prajapati story calls upon us to find a deeper meaning of giving, or giving up.

'And this deeper meaning of giving is not different from the deeper meaning of self-restraint and mercy which had dawned upon the gods and the demons.

'We as humans (we are also gods and demons) must not attribute real otherness to anything at all that we encounter.

'We are self-consciousness. If we were conscious of real, as opposed to merely apparent, otherness, that is, "not-selfhood", we would not be self-consciousness but "not-self-consciousness"!

'But is that our experience? We don't lose our sense of self-consciousness in our awareness of the diversity of world-appearance, do we?

'Nor is our root self-consciousness sharpened in any way when we are aware of our bodily forms, and we don't lose it when, as in deep sleep, we are devoid of any awareness of our bodily form.

'It would, however, be a mistake, for that reason, to regard our bodily form as not-selfhood, because in our awareness of it we don't lose self-consciousness.

'We must see all forms, including formless emptiness, as self-images of self, our own self-representations.

'Without a realisation of the many-centredness of ourselves, selfhood, we cannot be enthralled by existence and want the sport of life and civilisation on earth to continue indefinitely.

'Dear friends, it would be fair to say that the fundamental violence which Hinduism recognises is violence towards oneself, towards selfhood, self-consciousness.

'It is for this reason that non-violence cannot be anything other than self-realisation which was, not surprisingly, therefore, the self-confessed aim in life of that singular teacher of non-violence in our age, Mahatma Gandhi,' Babu concluded.

'Gandhi was no Mahatma, Professor Srivastava! He was a fraud who boasted that the partition of India would occur over his dead body, but did absolutely nothing to prevent it!' That was Dr Shrinivas Patwardhan's scream of dissent.

Pockets of people throughout the auditorium seemed to speak in hushed tones agreeing with Patwardhan.

Harenbhai and Subramaniam both got up to pacify Patwardhan, but Babu urged them to return to their seats, and responded to Patwardhan's calumny with deadly seriousness.

'Dr Shrinivas Patwardhan, you are a veteran freedom fighter and I salute you.

'But I put it to you that Gandhi's prophecy that the partition of India would occur over his dead body was substantially, if not literally, fulfilled by events.

'So long as Gandhi was alive, there was a permanent possibility of the people of India and Pakistan, as opposed to their power-hungry politicians, coming together in some form of partnership which would offer security to religious minorities throughout the subcontinent, thereby undoing partition as the reluctantly retreating British Empire had defined the term.

'It is only after his assassination that partition became unalterable, unmodifiable, actuality.

'Indian self-consciousness was violated, Indians and Pakistanis became "other" to one another. Ceasing to be self-conscious and becoming not-self-conscious, we have joined the mainstream of modern thought which has no use for the notion of self-consciousness. Only for consciousness which is always only conscious of something other than itself, of an environment of not-self-hood whose exploitation and despoliation causes modern humanity no moral qualms.

'Dr Patwardhan, I also put it to you that if Gandhi had undertaken a fast unto death to demand the withdrawal of the partition plan, the subcontinent would have been set on fire by communal vengefulness (and for the first time at the instigation of a saint) and in that fire India would have been cheated of independence, and her spiritual traditions would have lost credibility.

'India's political leaders would have had to beg the British Empire to continue to rule India.

'Mountbatten would have been delighted to do so, and Churchill would have demanded as a price for that service the division of India into two hundred small states.

'We would not have been able to think of Gandhi, or of you, Dr Patwardhan, as freedom fighters.

'Dr Patwardhan was on his feet shaking a fist, quite a contrast to the dancing Ramakrishna on the wall across the hall from him.

'Wait a little, Dr Patwardhan, I want to provoke you even more!' Babu thundered.

Pushpa and Gangaben and Gautam were tense, anticipating the victory of chaos over civility any moment, but they found Muniya calm.

Muniya looked over her shoulder and offered 'abhaya', reassurance, the gesture of a raised palm, to a troubled-looking George, who relayed the same message to a troubled-looking Harenbhai on the podium.

Subramaniam was scribbling notes on his pad for his report to the Bhavan's trustees on the evening's proceedings.

Violence And The Girl-Child

'Friends, I would like to provoke all of you a little more, and not only Dr Patwardhan, into deeper thought about Hinduism's vision of the foundations of violence, and I can't think of anything more suitable than Mahabharata evocations for achieving that purpose.

(Muniya smiled at Pushpa as if to say, 'I told you Babu would find a way out of the crisis, didn't I?' and Pushpa squeezed Muniya's hand in gratitude.)

'The Kurukshetra battle was won by the Pandavas. Barely, by the grace of Sri Krishna.'

Babu adopted the present tense to conform with a well-established tradition of sacred storytelling.

'It was Krishna who had tried hardest to prevent the war. Granting Dhritarashtra divine eyes, Krishna had shown the King his cosmic form (Arjuna was not the first to behold that form!), drawn attention to the justice of the Pandavas' modest demand for five villages as their inheritance, and to the inevitability of the destruction of all of Dhritarashtra's sons in war.

'But Dhritarashtra's answer to Krishna was that he preferred to be blind (blind to the avarice of his son Duryodhana), and war had become unavoidable.

'Arjuna's unexpected refusal, at the beginning of the Bhagavadgita, to fight a just war against his own relatives can be seen on a closer examination of the text and its context to be prompted by the perception that even relatives are "others". That there can be no guarantee that a fight may not start among the Pandavas who, although brothers, were still "other" than one another. Potential Karnas (the word Karna literally means "ear") who can hear the dualistic roar of samsara and be lured into jealousy of one another!

'Wars can be won, but even victors are losers to otherness! That is Arjuna's anguish! Not nerves!

'The Gita teaches Advaita, reveals to Arjuna that all forms are self-images of Atman, Krishna, his own deepest self, and that the unavoidable slaughter of that unavoidable war cannot be a sin against "others", there being none. But not fighting the war would be a sin against self, its omnipresent self-imaging.

'And yet, Krishna has had to break all rules of war himself to ensure a narrow victory for the Pandavas, thereby demonstrating that given the untameability of modern weaponry and the interdependence of modern societies (the Mahabharata is a modern story), even a just war cannot be fought justly, even if God were literally on your side, as he was with the Pandavas!

'It is wise, therefore, to remove the causes of conflict, and avoid war.

'Krishna's teaching of non-violence is a greater disincentive to war-making than doctrinaire pacifism can ever be!

'Let no one derive from the Bhagavadgita either the escapist idea that there can be no just war, nor the self-deceiving conclusion that even just wars can any more be fought justly! That is Krishna's teaching.

'Gandhi understood his teaching, but I think its full significance only dawned on him when, after the dropping of atomic bombs on innocent human beings in Hiroshima and Nagasaki, he declared that "now" we know that there can be no rules of war which war would not inevitably violate!

'But it would be a mistake to think that the Mahabharata's, Hinduism's, exploration of violence and its cure concludes with that extraordinary post-pacifist teaching of non-violence.

'The Kurukshetra war has ended. Years have rolled by. Krishna is back in Dvaraka. His own people, the Yadavas, have learned nothing from him. (What have India and Pakistan learned from the partition? What have European powers learned from the horrors of Auschwitz and Belsen and Hiroshima and Nagasaki?)

'A group of sages visit Dvaraka for a darshana of Krishna. Some Yadava youths decide to play a prank on the sages.

'Dressing up one of their male friends as a woman, making her look pregnant, they take her to the sages and ask them if they could predict the gender of the child that "woman" was going to give birth to.

'The sages see through the deception immediately, and what angers them is not the tomfoolery, harmless in itself, that is involved in the effrontery. What enrages them is the gender-preference for a male child that is implicit in the question they are asked to answer, the implied disrespect for the girl-child which continues unabated. Gender-identifying technology today enables families in India and elsewhere to destroy the girl-child in the womb through selective foeticide.

'The sages curse the Yadavas for their disrespect for the process of generativity, and predict that they would destroy themselves. And so they do.

'Krishna retires to a forest and lies down in yogic sleep. A hungry hunter, taking Krishna's beautiful form to be that of a deer, shoots an arrow at him and kills him.

> I would like to think that Krishna had actually become a deer and offered himself as legitimate food to a hunter who had no other way of feeding himself and his family.
>
> Krishna, Atman, self, is the deer and the hunter and the hunt.

'That is what, for Hinduism, makes it possible for there to be just life, the reduction of violence to the minimum taking of life which the necessity of survival requires.

'The ethics of non-violence derives its credibility from the metaphysics of non-duality.

'I would like to think that at the time of his self-sacrificial offering of himself (in the form of a deer) as food to a hungry being, Krishna would have recalled his childhood, full of fun, its unforgettability a sensuous correlate of the self-certitude of self-awareness.

'And would not Krishna have thought of his childhood in conjunction with the sacred memory of his biological mother Devaki, and his foster mother Yashoda?

'And would not the combination of the unforgettability of childhood and its companion femininity, which is motherhood, have made Krishna think of Radha, untameable girl-child in all stages of her life, as the perfect picture of Atman in the exteriority of experience, mirroring and enriching the self-certitude of selfhood in the interiority of self-consciousness?

'When we humiliate the girl-child, directly when we treat women unjustly, and indirectly when we mock generativity, as with our genetically mutilating nuclear weapons and the practice of selective female foeticide, don't we, like the foolish Yadava youths, invite the wrath of sages and annihilation?

'Dear friends, in all fairness to Dr Patwardhan, I must let you know that in his objections to my book *The Testimony of Janaka*, which he submitted in writing to the Bhavan, he had violently objected to my claim that Jnani Janaka would have refused to believe that Rama, avatara of Vishnu, could have banished Sita who, as a girl-child, was discovered by Janaka in the folds of self-realisation, as its perfect portrait.

'That Janaka in fact maintained that after the destruction of Ravana, Sita had reminded Rama of the unavoidable yet unecological killing of Maricha, a demon in a deer's disguise, by Rama, at her instigation.

'There was no way of avoiding killing Maricha, because the demon would have destroyed forest life, and it would have been impossible to battle Ravana without the support of forest life.

'And yet, although in disguise, Maricha was a deer. Rama, Sita, and Lakshmana had had their afternoon meal of venison, and there was no ecologically justified need to kill the deer.

'Sita suggested to Rama that to remind future humanity of the importance of observing the ecological code of honour, which forbids violence beyond the necessities of survival, they should separate in atonement for their unavoidable but indisputable violation of that code.

'Rama, you should protect culture in Ayodhya, and I, Sita, remaining in the forest, would be a custodian of nature,' she had suggested humorously, according to Babu's Janaka.

'A proposal which was immediately accepted by Maryada Purushottama Sri Rama.

'Priestly orthodoxy and male supremacists invented and interpolated into the Ramayana the idea of Rama banishing Sita from Ayodhya for her alleged infidelity during her incarceration in Lanka.

'Jnani Janaka had dismissed the suggestion that Sita would have merely wanted to be Rama's consort. Sita, like Rama, was incarnate self-realisation, and each was present in the other.

'My final contention in *The Testimony of Janaka* had been that the Ramayana began with the killing of one of a pair of birds in love-play by a hunter. And that it could poetically satisfactorily only end on a note of atonement for ecological wrongdoing.

'That Janaka had prophesied that the fate of the girl-child in India and the world would remain insecure until the truth of Sita's separation from Rama was rediscovered and their noble submission to ecological dharma internalised by humanity.

'Rama and Sita are the indivisibility of self-awareness. We cannot honour one and condemn the other without destroying the integrity of our own selfhood.

'Dr Patwardhan maintains that I have no right to read the

Ramayana or the Mahabharata in ways that suit my philosophical purposes.

'I maintain that I do. Vyasa was himself dissatisfied after writing the Mahabharata, and Narada Muni advised him to write the Bhagavatam, to narrate the pastimes of Krishna's childhood and bring femininity, as symbolised by Devaki and Yashoda and Radha, at least, to the forefront of his readers awareness.

'My study of Advaita Vedanta in Tiruvannamalai, accepting Sri Ramana Maharshi as my Guru, also left me unhappy, until I realised, by his grace, that I had to understand the spiritual and philosophical significance of the girl-child in our country and throughout the world.

'I would like to conclude my lecture with an appeal that I had made in *The Testimony of Janaka*.

'Hindus who believe that Rama did indeed banish Sita from Ayodhya cannot have the spiritual right to build a Rama temple in Ayodhya, without justifying the banishment of Sita.

'I believe this cannot be done. Because to justify the banishment of Sita from Ayodhya by Rama would tantamount to banishing from our own consciousness the most perfect picture of Atman that life reveals to us, that is, the girl-child. A denial of Atman, violence towards ourselves.

'Harenbhai, Shri Subramaniam, dear audience, I thank you for the opportunity you have given me to share thoughts with you on the theme "Hinduism and Violence" in these times of escalating intolerance which I believe can be countered with a deeper understanding of Hinduism's distinctive teaching and celebration of non-duality, Advaita.

'Aum Sri Ramanaya Namah.'

This concluded Babu's lecture.

Subramaniam called for a break of ten minutes and announced that Professor Ravi Srivastava would be happy to respond to questions and comments for half an hour after the break.

In the din of applause and hissing and catcalls, Babu heard the words, 'You did well, Babu!' in a familiar voice, deep within his heart.

Post-Pacifist Non-Violence

As they were settling back into their seats for the 'discussion' to begin, and to conclude, the lecture, Harenbhai informed Babu that in view of the likelihood of Babu being quite as exhausted as Harenbhai was, he had cancelled the post-lecture get-together with expatriate Indians at home over drinks and snacks which he had planned. After the lecture, unless Babu had other thoughts, they should call it a day and go home. Babu readily agreed, abandoning a naughty idea he had entertained earlier of taking Muniya out for dinner and a late night movie somewhere in Soho.

Without rising from his seat, Subramaniam vigorously waved inviting hands above his head and declared that Professor Srivastava would be happy to respond 'fully' to 'brief' questions and comments relevant to the lecture.

Harenbhai held his head between his heads, anticipating fireworks.

Muniya had pulled up her legs on her chair and sat in 'sukhasana', the 'easy sitting posture', silent, anticipating nothing.

Getting up with difficulty from his chair, Dr Patwardhan kicked off the discussion with a sneering question:

'Professor Srivastava, do you seriously believe that Indian independence was won non-violently? Isn't it time to bury the myth that it was?' he asked, looking around for supportive gestures from members of the audience, and there were many nods of approval cast in his favour.

Moving over to the lectern, Babu spoke slowly.

'I want to thank Dr Patwardhan for the brevity and precision of his important question. And I hope all of you will bear with what will unavoidably be a somewhat lengthy response to it.' A pleased Patwardhan sat down, confident that he had put Srivastava in the dock.

'Two million innocent human beings were sacrificed by the vivisection of India which is euphemistically called partition.

'And at least twenty times that number were uprooted from their ancient homelands in the subcontinent.

'It would be absurd to think that Indian freedom was "unaccompanied" by violence. But the demand for partition, which unleashed holocaust violence, was not a demand of the movement for India's freedom from British rule.

'Partition was a price extracted by the British Empire from India for daring to ask racist rule to "quit India", a blackmailing exercise which I am convinced the empire thought would lead to the abandoning of the demand for freedom even by Gandhi, at any rate to a grave embitterment of Hindu-Muslim relations, which had been evolving towards political and spiritual harmony over a period of centuries.

'The blackmail failed, but Indian independence was forcibly baptised in the blood of innocents.

'Dr Patwardhan, it is not Indian satyagraha for freedom, but the manner of British withdrawal which is tainted with horrific violence.

'However, it would be a profound error to think that the moral force which made India's demand for freedom undeniable was "pacifist non-violence".

'Gandhi's "Quit India" movement in 1942, quickly quelled though it was, was a warning that similar movements, non-violent but recurrent, would manifest all the time if British rule did not withdraw from India. And that these movements would have to be suppressed with the kind of brutality which Hitler had unleashed in Europe, thereby exposing the hollowness of the empire's claim to represent a higher level of civilisation than India's.

'India was astir with the thought that she had intervened in history against the institutionalised racism of British rule, which was not less objectionable than Nazi racism because it was less violent. Indeed, its systemic and, therefore, more enduring character made British racism in India no less loathsome than Nazi racism.

'It is perfectly reasonable to suppose that the Indian prisoners-of-war, taken captive by the Japanese, who formed Subhas Chandra Bose's "Indian National Army" in 1943, did so because of the moral inspiration of the Gandhi-led satyagraha for svaraj in mainland India.

'Bose's "Indian National Army" demonstrated that India had the capability to fight for her freedom in conventional, military ways, but chose a different path in India because she was engaged in an "experiment with truth", a search for a force greater than violence in resolving human conflicts.

'The INA's demonstration of Indian military capability (as opposed to terrorism) brought credibility to Indian satyagraha, making its non-violence the non-violence "of the brave", as opposed to the non-violence of the weak which Gandhi had always decried.

'Gandhi and Bose may not themselves have been fully aware of this collaboration of their movements for the emergence of the possibility of "post-pacifist" non-violence.

'Dr Patwardhan, I would like to respond to your question succinctly with the thought that Indian freedom was attained not by fundamentalist, pacifist non-violence, but by revolutionary, post-pacifist ahimsa, which demands nurturing, not burial.

'Dr Patwardhan announced that he was walking out in protest against Professor Srivastava's eccentric reading of history which was of a piece with his eccentric reading of mythology.

There was not much support for Patwardhan this time, because many in the audience who thought of Gandhi and Bose as incompatible figures in the history of India's struggle for freedom were happy to be reminded of their unexpected complementarity.

Bose's 'hissing' had made it unnecessary for Gandhian non-violence to 'bite'.

The Third Atom Bomb

Babu noticed that sitting in the back rows of the auditorium, towards the right, was a small group of ascetic looking people, very probably English and pacifist and socialist, and that one of them, a thin but wirily strong middle-aged woman, looked extremely agitated. She caught his eye and rose and spoke with fervour.

'Professor (she omitted the difficult-to-pronounce sound "Srivastava", causing Muniya to whisper into Pushpa's ear a protest against the unfair distribution of the labour of correct pronunciation of foreign words in the world), I am amazed that you have so far said absolutely nothing at all about the shameful testing and acquisition of nuclear weapons by India, the land of the Buddha and Gandhi. Does Hinduism condone the possession and possible use of such weapons? Do you?' she asked icily, the clear accents of her pure English speech bringing to her complaint a biting edge of indignation.

'What about Pakistan?' somebody asked her, and a number of people in the audience targeted her with complaints about the double standards used by western critics of India's newly acquired nuclear capability. She looked like a minority of one in an overwhelmingly pro-Indian crowd, and Subramaniam rightly raised his voice and reminded the audience that the lady's remarks were addressed to Professor Srivastava, and that he alone should respond to them.

Babu raised both his arms and requested silence and an opportunity for him to talk to the lady who had just spoken, and reminded everybody that she had a right to her opinion in the matter.

'Dear friend,' he said, addressing her gender-indifferently, 'You have obviously forgotten the Mahabharata story I told a while ago of the sages who were asked by a group of young men to predict the gender of the baby that was going to be born, so they claimed, to a male friend of theirs whom they had dressed up to look like a pregnant woman. This prank was seen through and regarded by the sages as a gross insult to the sanctity of human reproductivity, and they laid a curse of collective death upon the clan to which the young men belonged, the clan, as it happened, of God-incarnate Krishna himself. And the curse was fulfilled.

'Hinduism cannot condone the acquisition of nuclear weapons by anyone, nor do I, as a Hindu and as a freethinking individual human being.

'But I put it to you, dear friend, that the brutal and avoidable vivisection of the living subcontinent of India by the British Empire in 1947, and the holocaust which was unleashed by that splitting of the spiritual unity of an ancient and enduring civilisation, is completely analogous to the splitting of the material unity of the atom which was involved in the atomic bombing of Hiroshima and Nagasaki by America in 1945, with the full support of Britain.

'The partition of India is "the third atom bomb", to speak analogically but not for that reason untruthfully or unilluminatingly, with which western powers have destroyed masses of innocent human beings in pursuit of their political and economic interests.

'The fallout of the third bomb, unlike that of the first two, continues. Hindus and Muslims continue to hate and kill one another in wars between India and Pakistan which are provoked by the inherently irrational splitting of the subcontinent.

'Shameful as it is, the acquisition of nuclear weapons by India and Pakistan is yet an act of confession by Hindus and Muslims of the deep, genetic, hatred of one another which the reality of partition often arouses in them.

'Once the confessional nature of their nuclear capability is understood by the people of India and Pakistan, atonement will be in sight.

'Perhaps in Kashmir, which retains something of the undivided character of the Indian subcontinent, a cultural parliament could be instituted within existing sovereignties, to which members would be elected from the subcontinent as a whole, not to rule but serve the land and all its traditions indivisibly.

'The souls of the two million human beings slaughtered by partition would receive through that process of atonement their long delayed last rites.

'And dear friend, let me tell you why I think no one has any right whatever to possess a single nuclear weapon.

'A nuclear weapon cannot be made without an assessment of its destructive capability in relation to the Hiroshima and Nagasaki bombs. It cannot be invested with terrorising power without such a comparative assessment.

> And this cannot be done without reference to the shame suffered by the victims of the Hiroshima and Nagasaki bombings, the shame of knowing that their descendants are liable to genetic deformation till eternity ....

'I believe that a serious violation of a fundamental human right is involved in this reference (to the shame of being the unique and targeted victims of weapons of genetic mutilation) which the manufacture and possession and testing of nuclear weapons cannot avoid.

'Because the shame in question is a unique humiliation, a wound which cannot be bared at all without the permission of all the descendants of the Hiroshima and Nagasaki victims, the majority of whom are not yet born.

'The right of these victims to prohibit reference to their humiliation is not disanalogous to an intellectual property right. Because every moment of life lived by them brings to their condition the status of a positive, original, construction: the status of an intellectual property.

'There is not enough wealth in the world to compensate for the violation of this right to the integrity of life, no consent can be wide enough to include distant sufferers.

'We must heal the wounds caused by the three bombs, dear friend, and not play the blame game.

'Aum Sri Ramanaya Namah.'

Babu returned to his seat, sweating profusely.

Untouchability And The Mandukya Upanishad

An anxious Subramaniam asked Babu if he was feeling all right, and was willing to take more questions, or did he want the meeting to be wound up and rest for a while in his office? If necessary, a doctor could be called to examine him.

Harenbhai suggested the latter course of action, nervously, and there was a moment of anxiety shared by the audience as Muniya came running to the podium, looked at Babu and found him smiling at her 'like her'. That was sufficient reassurance for her that all was well with him and whispering into Subramaniam's and Harenbhai's ears that Babu would be comfortable with one last question, she scampered back to her place next to Pushpa like a gilehri.

'A last, brief, question, before we end this evening's programme, friends,' Subramaniam announced.

Babu drank some water and walked back to the lectern.

'Yes, friends, let's have the last word!' he joked, and everybody laughed, relieved that their lecturer was well.

After a long pause, which caused Subramaniam to begin to rise to declare the meeting closed, a raised hand was spotted by Babu and he requested its owner to speak, and Subramaniam reverted to his seated position.

'I am D. Nagaraj,' the speaker said, 'An untouchable Sanskrit scholar from South India. Could you, Professor Srivastava, locate for me some definitive thought in the Vedic corpus which specifically discredits Hinduism's violent and ancient and unabated practice of untouchability against a mass of its own adherents?' the questioner asked pointedly, and sceptically, and sat down with a grave face, which evinced little hope of his question receiving a satisfactory answer.

'Yes I can, Nagarajji. By Guru's grace my attention is drawn to the Mandukya Upanishad, where the sacred syllable "Aum" is identified with Atman and Brahman, and is declared to be "chatushpat", that is, "four-footed".

'It is a matter of deep regret that even so great an authority as Adi Shankaracharya, in his commentary on Gaudapada's Mandukya Karika, interprets the word chatushpat, as it occurs in the Mandukya Upanishad, to mean a coin of commercial currency, four-sided as it is in its own way, and not in its straightforward sense of something four-footed.

'Like a cow or any other four-footed animal, or somebody who has been knocked down from his or her station of bipedality to a crawling, four-footed, condition of bondage, such as members of the "fourth" caste have been by caste orthodoxy.

'Nagarajji, the possibly adivasi sage "Manduka" (frog), from whose name is derived the title "Mandukya" of the Upanishad we are talking about, is drawing coded attention to the high symbolic status of four-footed animal life, and felled, caste-oppressed, humanity: the status of "being on all fours", of being harmonised like the three states of consciousness (the waking, dream, and sleep states) in the pervasive, fourth, "turiya", dimension of consciousness which is self-awareness.

'Nagarajji, how can it be possible for a sannyasin like Adi Shankaracharya to identify "Aum", ultimate reality, with a coin which bears the image of a temporal sovereign, and which is the very shape of an object of greed?'

'I am convinced caste-orthodoxy has interpolated the

interpretation attributed to Shankaracharya, so as to prevent readers and hearers of the Mandukya Upanishad from encountering sage Manduka's celebration of non-human and ostracised human life.

'And his revolutionary reminder that those whom we call the "fourth" varna are, indeed, the symbol of the harmony between the one and the many which is the miraculous reality of Atman and Brahman.'

'Chatushpat, Aum. Worthy of worship, not ill-treatment.'

'Ramana Maharshi used to say that God or Atman alone is untouchable and invisible. Those whom we think of as untouchables and invisibles (insisting on their wearing bells round their necks to warn us of their proximity to us so as to enable us not to look at them!) are, therefore, worthy of worship!'

'Nagarajji, the Mandukya Upanishad is the canonical scripture of explicitly trans-anthropocentric and non-exploitative Advaita.

'For all we know, adivasi sage Mandukya may have found in the folds of forest bushes a "four-footed", crawling, girl-child, a Sita of forest life, a perfect picture of Atman, and he may have heard from her the sacred sound "Aum".

'Aum Sri Ramanaya Namah.'

Amidst much celebratory noise, Subramaniam thanked everybody and declared the meeting closed.

The auditorium emptied slowly and Babu and Muniya took a while to emerge out of its doors, only to find Dr Shrinivas Patwardhan and the frail but fanatical English pacifist lady waiting to have a go at Babu. With accusatory fingers targeting him, the two of them simultaneously informed Babu that he had not dealt with their questions adequately at all.

They would have gladly engaged him in more infructuous debate for several more hours had Muniya not angrily intervened to say, 'Can't you see he's tired!'

George miraculously materialised and steered the Desai guests skilfully out of the auditorium's foyer and led them to the Rolls Royce in the Bhavan's parking lot and drove them back to Russell Square.

Babu was certainly tired, not merely physically but also psychically, because the lecture had involved journeying backwards and forwards, in time and truth, to portray Hinduism's understanding of violence in philosophical, non-simplistic terms, beyond the superficialities of doctrinaire militarism and pacifism.

Babu looked at Muniya's face in the mirror of the lift which took them up to the Desai flat, and the lightning-quick movement of her eyes and mouth which it reflected comforted him deeply. 'You did well, Babu!' Muniya said and laughed.

'Thank you, gilehri, for your prayers and ceaseless vigilance during the lecture, guiding my thoughts along favourable directions,' was Babu's truthful response to Muniya's appreciation of his efforts.

Babu and Muniya were allowed to eat alone, as Harenbhai wanted to spare Babu any further strain of speaking, and they retired to their separate rooms.

Before long, however, there was a knock on Babu's door. Harenbhai wanted to know what he and Muniya wanted to do the next day, as they were scheduled to fly to Mumbai the day after.

Muniya came out of her room, combing her hair, to be a part of the deliberations.

'Harenbhai, I would have loved to take Muniya to the Isle of Skye in the Scottish Highlands, had we any time left. It was there, during a blizzard in 1966, that I had the clear thought that modern western philosophy and science do not possess the conceptual and ethical resources to guide humanity to safety across the ocean of uncertainty and despair in which it is now drifting,' Babu said with real sadness in his voice, both for humanity and for his own limited time with Muniya.

And then a thought occurred to Babu and he spoke excitedly.

'Harenbhai, I want to see and show Muniya the Gandhi mural which I believe has been installed inside Oxford's oldest church, St Mary's.

'We'll take the afternoon train and be back before dinner. What do you say Muniya?'

'Done!' is what she said, as did Harenbhai.

Gandhi Mural, St Mary's Church, Oxford

Sankeertana In Oxford

It was early afternoon and an unexpectedly clear day when Babu and Muniya arrived in Oxford from Paddington by a fast train.

Babu took Muniya to St Mary's, and asked someone who looked like a church porter (Oxford porters wield great authority) if it was true that St Mary's had a Gandhi mural.

'Up those winding steps, on your right,' was the precise, unelaborated answer.

Babu and Muniya climbed the staircase and exactly where the porter had indicated was the Gandhi mural: Gandhi seated on his knees, wearing John Lennon spectacles (he did wear steel-rimmed spectacles), both his arms raised in the air!

'Babu, what do you think the mural's message is?' Muniya asked.

'Darling girl, I am afraid the message is dark. Gandhi seems to be raising his arms like Vyasa in the Mahabharata, lamenting that no one sees that war in our times is uncontainable, even if it is just.'

Muniya shook her head in respectful disagreement.

'Babu, I think the mural indicates Gandhi's desire to break into sankeertana dance, and draws attention to his inability to do so in our times!' was Muniya's reading of the image.

And Babu's gilehri swung into a devotional dance movement, adapted to modern dance rhythms, and started to descend the winding church staircase, chanting Chaitanya Mahaprabhu's mantra, 'Hare Rama Hare Rama Hare Rama Hare Hare, Hare Krishna Hare Krishna Hare Krishna Hare Hare!'

A small group of amused onlookers had gathered at the foot of the stairs, and a visibly embarrassed Babu descended the stairs with Muniya.

Babu was amazed, and quickly overjoyed, to find that some of the onlookers joined Muniya in the celebratory Rama-Krishna dance and it was a post-modern theological pop-group led by Muniya which wound its way out of the church.

In the courtyard outside, Muniya introduced Babu to her fellow dancers.

'This is Professor Ravi Srivastava, he will answer all your questions on the Gandhi mural and on Rama and Krishna, but he will not dance!' she declared, amidst laughter.

'Muniya grossly exaggerates my capabilities,' is all that Babu could say.

One of the dancers was a serious Christian who was doing a comparative study of Christian bhakti and Vaishnavism.

'Wasn't Gandhi's favourite Vaishnava hymn different, though, "Vaishnava jana to tene kahiye je peeda parayee jane re", he asked Babu, revealing how rapidly inter-faith theological curiosity was spreading around the world.

'You are absolutely right, my friend. Gandhi would encourage his Christian associates to modify that hymn slightly and sing, "Christiana jana to tene kahiye je peeda parayee jane re",' Babu informed him.

'How interesting, how very interesting,' said the scholar of comparative religion, and exchanged addresses with Babu.

Confession

It was mid-September and beginning to get cold in England, and Babu and Muniya, wearing light woollens (he had a coarse Haryana shawl thrown over his shoulders, she wore a light woollen pullover 'inside' her denim shirt, a common practice among students in Britain even during Babu's Aberdeen days), walked with linked arms to a Greek café down an alley off High Street, ready for something to eat and hot tea.

Before entering the alley, Babu pointed out the various ancient colleges that dotted the street: Brasenose, All Souls, University College, the Queens' College, and asked Muniya why her Baba hadn't suggested that she go to Oxford or Cambridge, instead of Santa Barbara on the west coast of America.

'Babu, why didn't "you" go to Oxford or Cambridge?' was Muniya's counter-question.

'I won a scholarship to go to Aberdeen, which suited me, because I wanted a certain distance from mainstream Oxford philosophy, so as to retain scepticism regarding modern western philosophy as a whole. You could call it prejudice, but it was more pride, I think,' Babu explained.

'I think your pride or prejudice must have influenced Baba,

because when I won a scholarship to Santa Barbara, he reminded me of your preference for a distance from mainstream Englishness. 'Babu, do you hate the English?' Muniya asked as the two tourists sat down at a corner table in the Greek café, and quickly ordered what was Babu's favourite English food: baked beans on toast with tomatoes (and French fries too, please, insisted Muniya), to be followed by the hottest tea that could be served.

'Good heavens, no, dear girl,' Babu declared, wiping his spectacles which had steamed up in the heated café.

'I must tell you what I forgot to tell Baba and Archana twenty years ago after an altercation between me and an English friend of Baba's, I think his name was Mark Smith.

'Smith had declared that he was a vegetarian, and then he lit a cigarette. I asked him how he could be both a vegetarian and a smoker, because by smoking he was hurting an animal, that is, himself! Smith had flared up, thinking I was an Indian racist who was denying an Englishman the status of a human being and thinking of him as an animal! It was very funny indeed.

'That argument against smoking was actually used against me (I was a heavy smoker then, and a vegetarian) by an English friend ages ago. I have never ceased to admire the eccentric genius of the English.

'My complaint against their empire in India has always been that it was devoid of real eccentricity. British rulers of India should have taught themselves Sanskrit and Persian and Arabic, or at least Hindi and Urdu, and, playing real kabaddi with India, find with Indians a larger, limitless, identity!' Babu concluded, but found Muniya fixing him with a stare.

She had not paid close attention to what he was saying, because she wanted to ask him right then the question she had wanted to ask him at the airport in San Francisco. After rehearsing the question in her mind, she let it out, at last!

'Babu, why did you visit us in Pune only once after your first visit in 1984?

'It must have been in 1987, when you came the second time. Ayi was trying to get me used to the idea of wearing a uniform throughout the ten long years that I would be at Sanawar, the residential school in the Himalayan foothills where Baba was determined to send me. She was forcing me to wear the uniform when you came into the house with Baba.'

'Yes, I remember the scene,' Babu interrupted Muniya's reverie with his own. 'The blue shirt, grey skirt and stockings, and the blazer, yes, Muniya, you looked like a pigeon that was about to soar into the sky of freedom, not a child being readied for the regimented life of a boarding school. I was so happy to see you! Brave Muniya, you didn't cry when Arun took you to the station from where he would take you by train to Delhi and then on to Kalka and then by road to Sanawar. Archana stayed back to be with Abhinava, who was only five, Kalpana was still there in the house. I returned to Kolkata before Arun returned.'

Babu suddenly fell silent, and Muniya too, and they ate their beans on toast with tomatoes and French fries broodingly, and that's when the jukebox blared out Paul McCartney's haunting number 'Yesterday'.

'So Babu, why didn't you come to see me during the many summer vacations when I was home in Pune? Yes, I have not forgotten that you telephoned Baba frequently, and always asked to speak to me. "Do well, Muniya," you would say, and insist on my telling you to do well too! What "were" you doing, Babu?'

Muniya couldn't have been more blunt in her interrogation of Ravi Srivastava.

As they sipped hot tea, Babu made an astonishing confession to Muniya.

'Muniya, gilehri, I was trying to be a brahmachari, and at the same time reading all I could on Sri Ramakrishna and Sri Sarada and Svami Vivekananda.'

'I didn't believe there was anything wrong with being married or with sexual love, no! But I was absolutely certain that in no woman would I find the magical light of undeniable reality that I had found in you, as a direct result of my prayer to my guru, I am convinced! And without that light, I would find sexual or married love wanting in truth.

'But I worried too much about the world and could not become a sannyasin.

'Muniya, lest you think I am asexual or homosexual, I must confide in you that when I was a student in Aberdeen, a beautiful Scottish sculptress and I had kept each other warm through winter nights.

'But she thought it odd of me to be uncomfortable with the many-centredness of her love life and I drifted away from that relationship.

'And when I returned to India, I had a live-in relationship with a brilliant academic who, however, thought it odd of me to want to go off to Tiruvannamalai every weekend, and pronounced me a fake sannyasin and a failed householder and literally closed the door of her house on me.

'I returned to Tiruvannamalai for undistracted study and sadhana, and didn't think I would be able to love again.

'But Ramana revealed to me that the feminine child was the most luminous portrait of Atman. And then I had your darshana.

'And I cannot now block out of my mind the reality of female humanity and I don't mean only its childhood form,' Babu concluded.

Babu was amazed and relieved to find that Muniya was looking at him not with anger but with pity.

She walked up to the jukebox and played Louis Armstrong's evergreen number 'What a wonderful world!' to cheer up Babu and to confront him with the possibility that while the brahmachari may successfully renounce sexuality, he certainly loses a sense of this wonderful world which is sustained by erotic and romantic love. 'How did Muniya know that that Armstrong number was my favourite song?' Babu wondered, convinced that events were being driven by destiny.

'Muniya, the thought of you growing up without losing the light of childhood's image of self-realisation has sustained me all these years in my brahmacharya, imperfect though it has been,' Babu said when Muniya returned to their table.

'I love you, Muniya!'

Babu's confession was complete.

'Do you love me, gilehri?' Babu asked her nervously.

'Immensely, but in my own way. Babu, I have lots of questions for you about the brahmacharya of Ramakrishna and Gandhi, but we'll leave that for later,' said Muniya, as she and Babu boarded the evening train back to London.

Muniya was sleepy and slept with her head on Babu's shoulders nearly all the way to Paddington, letting her cobra pigtail fall over his shoulder with a smile of compassion.

For Babu, the proximity unmasked his consuming desire for Muniya, and not only his love for her, beyond all doubt and rationalising self-deception.

Good old George received them and drove them to the Desai home for a light meal and an early night.

Babu could not pretend that he could switch off the lights in his room and drift into sleep. He sat at a desk and wrote a note for Muniya.

Pyari Muniya,

You are the only woman I have known for whom I have felt, simultaneously, both the paternal protectiveness of a Raja Janaka, Sita's father, and his understandable desire that only the bravest and noblest prince in all the worlds should win her love, 'and' the unrecorded desire of some unmarried shudra servant in Janaka's household who had watched Sita grow into matchless beauty and luminosity from early childhood and who, despite his years, had prayed that love for him may awaken in her heart and that she might choose him as the servant of her body and life till his dying day.

Muniya, you could leave me standing underneath the ambivalent Gandhi mural and descend to solid ground to find Arjuna, the most glorious of the five Pandava princes, waiting on his horse or in his limousine outside the church to carry off his Satyabhama (she of lustrous passion for truth, you!) to a life of rightful fulfilment of youth's desire.

Or, you could let me follow you down the winding steps of non-linear time and find another ground and celebrate with me a life of non-dualist, non-ageist, love, with humour and the confidence that I will look at no other woman than you and dissolve my separateness in you before my body dissolves its separateness in death.

I don't want you right now to do anything more than receive this petition of love in the court of your heart, putting it away in the folds of the Francis Bacon book I have given you, letting a testimony of hope and love coexist between portraits of decay and despair.

But you have only three months before you return to Santa Barbara and confront your viva committee again. Ask me all the questions you want to about Hinduism and India, war and peace, illumination and annihilation, sexuality and brahmacharya, religion and secularism, and I will do my best to bring to you whatever I have been able to understand about these grave subject-matters by the grace of Appa and Muniya!

Always, your own Babu.

Babu slipped this note under Muniya's door and went to sleep. And found a note slipped under his door, when he woke up.

Dearest Babu.

Be at peace with the impulses of your heart. I know and respect them.

More later, love, Muniya.

Last Meal With The Desais

Lunch at the Desai home for Babu and Muniya was going to be their last time together with the whole family, as they were scheduled to catch the evening Air India flight to Mumbai, and would need to leave in time for the elaborate security checks that were now in place at all international airports: George was to drive them to Heathrow.

Harenbhai sat at one end and opposite him, Babu, with Pushpa and Gautam on one side, and Gangaben and Muniya (whose jet-black hair, washed early in the morning, fell over her shoulders in great waves) on the other side of the dining table.

Aware that her flowing black hair might cause Babu to think that she had assumed that aspect of Kali's form to admonish him for his candour, Muniya turned and smiled at him. A greatly relieved Babu thanked Harenbhai and Gangaben for their hospitality and support, and apologised for not being able to bring any souvenirs for the family from Oxford, rushed as their visit had been.

As they reached the last stage of the lunch, a relaxed final round of fresh filter coffee, Pushpa asked Babu for a gift. 'Ravi Sabeb,' she said, 'I would greatly treasure the gift of a story, a

Ramayana story, a story about Sita, from you, canonical or apocryphal, mainstream or interpolated by the enlightenment of sages or the bhakti of devotees.'

A murmur of endorsement of Pushpa's request emanated collectively from all members of the Desai family, and even Muniya, transferring her waterfall hair from her shoulders to her back in a gesture of encouragement, said, 'Yes Babu, let's hear a Sita story.'

Babu closed his eyes and his inner ears heard Muniya's command, 'Do well!' and commenced his story.

'Sita, her very name means "of the furrows", was the girl-child of Raja Janaka, who was a jnani, found in the furrows of freshly, lightly, non-violently ploughed land. A jnani is a self-realised sage, one who is ceaselessly self-aware, not aware of "not-self" anywhere at all.

'I think the idea of freshly, lightly, non-violently, ploughed land conveys the ethical and ecological sensitivity of a jnani's life, the "furrows" of such a life the illumined interstices of a sage's brain.

'There, in the sacred folds of illumination, Janaka found a girl-child, Sita.

'I would like to think that Sita, aware of the fate of the girl-child in our society, would have been a luminous baby who yet refused to speak for a long time, exhibiting also thus the power of "mouna", silence, a characteristic worthy of a child adopted by a sage.

'And yet Janaka would have been worried, the thought that his radiant daughter might be mute would have troubled him. "Which prince would consent to marry a mute girl, even if she became the most dazzlingly beautiful young woman in all three worlds?"

'Pushpa, I would like to think that Janaka would have sought the help of a shudra servant in his court who, following Janaka's example, had devoted all his life to meditation on Atman, without neglecting his duties.

'This servant-sadhaka would have sat on the floor near Sita's baby-bed and told her stories, refusing to accept as real or irreversible her stubborn, apparent, speechlessness.

'And he would have told her this story, told in our own times by Sri Ramakrishna Paramahamsa, which would have brought forth speech from Sita's sorrowing heart.

'Blessed babygirl,' he would have begun. 'A firefly was distressed by her tiny light compared to the bright lights of countless stars in the night sky, and by the dazzling light of the round and radiant moon. Suddenly clouds appeared and hid the stars and the moon and a breeze started to blow. The firefly leapt into the current, sailing up and down, right and left. Pride entered her heart, she thought she was the light of the world, banisher of darkness.

'The breeze grew stronger and the stars were once again visible, and their brightness and manyness made the firefly despondent again. The stars are the light of the world, not me, a miserable little firefly, she thought.

'But then pride entered the hearts of the stars and they thought they were the light of the world, banishers of darkness. The wind grew stronger still and clouds once again hid the stars, but a brilliant moon burrowed its way out of them and the firefly thought it was the moon, despite the spots on its face, which was the light of the world, banisher of darkness. Alas, in pride, the moon also thought so, and clouds devoured the moon!

'Then it rained and rained through the night. The firefly thought it was the end of the world and slept in a little niche in the wall of a temple.

'The rain stopped as dawn broke and the sky cleared. An orange playful sun awakened the firefly with a ray of its light. Some stars and the moon, pale and contrite, were still visible in th sky. The sun addressed comforting words to them.

'My dear firefly, stars and moon, listen to me. When I rest, the moon does my duty. When clouds hide the moon, stars do my duty, guiding all travellers through life's journey. And when clouds cover the stars too, then beloved firefly, you are guided by your own light. You are like me, self-luminous. But don't be vain again. It is in cooperation with one another that we help life traverse day and night. And don't blame the darkness too much. Without it we would not be visible at all!

'Pushpa, the shudra's story would have awakened self-realisation in Sita's heart, brought hope for the girl-child, and for all oppressed and silenced beings. She would have uttered some words. The Gayatri mantra itself, I should think, which was supposedly revealed first to Rama's preceptor Vishvamitra. But I have no doubt Sita was the first to chant the mantra, honouring the sun for imaging the self-luminosity of Atman.'

'Perhaps the shudra's name was "Ravi",' Pushpa suggested, and all laughed.

And as the lift took Babu and Muniya down later, Babu said to Muniya: 'Pyari Muniya, I didn't complete the story. The shudra remained desperately in love with Sita throughout his life.'

Conception

George pulled the Rolls out of the Russell Square area down central London streets and, negotiating heavy traffic skilfully, mounted the Heathrow motorway. Soon the vehicle achieved the humming sound of 'being on the way'.

That is when Muniya, sitting in the passenger seat next to George, and Babu in solitary splendour in the rear, simultaneously realised how much they were going to miss the brief but hectic time they had shared in London, and felt gratitude for the considerateness and wisdom with which George had dealt with tricky situations during the lecture at the Bharatiya Vidya Bhavan. Simultaneously, and therefore unintelligibly, they thanked George for all that he had done for them, causing him to brake suddenly, as he thought that they had left something behind in the Desai apartment and would like to be driven back to retrieve it.

'Sorry for startling you, George, we were only saying "thank you" to you,' explained Muniya to a greatly relieved George. Babu stuttered in search of suitable words of contrition to add to Muniya's plain "sorry!" but Muniya turned back and frowned to say, 'That's enough, Babu, please!'

'Control my life, Muniya!' Babu said to himself. He had not heard blunt words of such sweet authority ever before.

But before Babu could slip into self-indulgent, self-pitying, reverie, George addressed a question to him, with Muniya smiling at him this time, urging him to listen carefully to George's query.

'Professor Srivastava, as I think I mentioned to you before, I have returned to my Catholic Christian faith, without abandoning my love for Sri Krishna, because I found Iskcon religiosity as organised as I had known Catholic Christianity to be, and I thought I should return to the devil I knew better!' George said, exploding in self-lampooning laughter which delighted Muniya and amused Babu, bringing to him also a measure of self-knowledge.

'I don't think I have the youthful capacity for laughter which Muniya admires,' he realised, with a twinge of jealousy for George which he soon overcame, not through humorous acknowledgement of the endurance of ego in old age, but less admirably by his adult sense of the unworthiness of jealousy.

'Yes, George, I remember your telling us about that during our visit to the Tate Gallery,' Babu said. 'We cannot cut ourselves off from our roots, and don't have to. Truth is its own foundation, its roots are in the sky, as Krishna himself reminds us in the Gita. Exchanging one set of roots for another can make us forget the sovereignty of truth.'

'Yes, of course, Professor. But I am deeply troubled by the Catholic Church's teaching that the use of contraceptives during sexual intercourse is wrong under all circumstances. Could you throw some light on this question? I could not have bought up this subject if Mr Desai had also been here.'

That was George's urgent, practical, dilemma, and he looked nervously at Muniya and resumed his driving. Muniya remained rock-carved, waiting for Babu to give serious thought to the question, which troubled her too.

'George and Muniya,' Babu said, surprising both by this joint mode of address, but they quickly understood that Professor Ravi Srivastava was about to hold forth for the benefit of the younger generation of humanity as a whole, and heard Babu's reflections on the subject with close and amused attention!

'George and Muniya,' Babu repeated, 'We must first ask ourselves if our conception of a human being, ourselves, is adequate, before we can criticise or defend practices like contraception, that is, the attempted prevention of the conception of new human life during sexual intercourse.

'We are not merely this human form, nor is it that we are not this form at all. We are self-awareness, which images itself in all forms, human and non-human, in all beings and nothingness too.

'If we conceive of ourselves in this non-dualist way, and the ripeness of such conception is what self-realisation comes to, it will become clear to us that biological reproductivity can be a celebration of the replicability of self-realisation. The significance of the continuity of life, the worthwhileness of living, can become clearer to us.

'But the need to limit the size of our own communities and species will be a corollary of such a realisation, and the idea of the practice of contraception during sexual intercourse will no longer appear to be something inherently unnatural,' Babu inferred, and paused, because he noticed that George was getting really excited by this line of thought and Babu didn't want this excitement to distract his driving.

'The pleasure of sexuality is grounded in the joy of the singularity of self-awareness which is also the many-centrednes of its self-images.

'A non-dualist conception of ourselves, which would be a celebration of this joy at the heart of reality, can help liberate the idea of sexual pleasure in caring and committed erotic love which is not, however, biologically reproductive, from the guilt and superficiality which surround it.

'But George and Muniya, for that very reason, the tradition of celibacy or brahmacharya, honoured in many spiritual traditions, including Catholic Christianity, would also be seen not as deprivation or denial but as the same search for and celebration of the joy of reality.

'Sexual love and pleasure and brahmacharya in caring and

compassionate lives will then be seen as complementary sadhanas of self-realisation, not contradictory impulses of the unredeemed human heart,' Babu concluded.

George was comforted by Babu's advaitin reflections on the complementarity of sexuality and brahmacharya and the conception of ourselves, and pulled up at a petrol station to make some notes in his diary.

Babu and Muniya stepped out of the car to stretch their legs.

George indicated with a grin to Babu that he had jotted down the main points of the latter's disquisition on conception and contraception, and that they should be on their way again to Heathrow. But just as the three strapped themselves into their seats, and George was about to set sail again, his cell phone rang.

Law-abidingly George took the call while the Rolls was still stationary, and was greeted by the voice of Gautam Desai, Harenbhai's son, at the other end, who wanted to have a word with Professor Srivastava.

'Certainly, Gautam, here he is!' said George, and passed the phone to Babu and started the vehicle. Gautam and Babu had a long conversation on the phone.

Gautam: 'Professor Srivastava, there is a question which I had wanted to raise during the lecture but did not, because you looked very tired, and there wasn't enough time at home to do so. May I do so now, briefly, if you don't mind being chased like this?'

Babu: 'It will be my pleasure to hear and respond to your question, Gautam. Let's have a good chase, chasing truth!'

(Muniya was all attention, and held Babu's left hand encouragingly with her right hand for a moment and then withdrew it, but not her gaze from his, face. Babu closed his eyes to hear Gautam better but then opened them again to be empowered by Muniya's still but radiant face.)

Gautam: 'Professor Srivastava, along with many of my friends, I feel that Mahatma Gandhi's decision to hand over the reins of political authority to the Hinduism-ignorant Jawaharlal Nehru after independence, instead, for instance, to a believing Hindu like

Sardar Patel, was an act which has proved disastrous for India and Hinduism.

'I would be grateful to hear your response to this assessment of Gandhi's judgement, Professor Srivastava, especially as I was shaken out of complacent thinking about the relationship between Gandhi and Subhas Chandra Bose on which you threw interesting light during the lecture.'

Babu: 'Gautam, I have given some thought to this question and I am grateful for this opportunity to share my understanding of it with you.

'Gandhi and Nehru held very divergent views about the path of social and cultural and economic development that was best for India to follow after independence, that is true.

'But Gautam, Gandhi was an observant politician. He met thinking people from all over the world, he was not insulated from world opinion.

'I think he would have realised that, like Nehru, most relatively young people (under fifty or sixty years of age) around the world, including India, were socialist by persuasion, and impressed by the Soviet experiment of heavy industrialisation and state control of all means of production.

'Nehru was such a person, a moderate socialist and a charismatic leader whom the radical communist movement in India in the late 1940s would have loved to use to come to power and implement a violent revolution, such as was being done in China by Mao Tse-Tung.

'The cost of such a revolution to India as a whole and not only Hinduism would have been even more catastrophic than the cost of partition. It would have been the cost of the so-called cultural revolution which China had to bear, the destruction of the non-renewable resources of spiritual culture.

'Gandhi may have felt that the likelihood of such violence would increase if Nehru, denied political authority, were to join hands with the revolutionary communist movement in India which was waiting in the wings to capture political power around independence. He may have had the prescience to understand that under the moderate leadership of a Nehru, India would be in a position to judge for herself what works and what doesn't under socialism.

'And this has indeed happened, thanks to Gandhi's apparently irrational but profoundly responsible and wise decision to bequeath political authority to Nehru, with whom he had serious philosophical differences, and not to more like-minded people like Patel or Rajagopalachari who were, however, less charismatic than Nehru and much older.

'Modernism, socialist or capitalist, cannot, as a result, tempt India to abandon her cultural and spiritual resources.

'Gautam, I think Gandhi deserves gratitude, not censure, for his far-sighted decision to let Nehru try out his ideas. An experiment with truth, so to speak, which has been very instructive.'

Gautam: 'Professor Srivastava, this is a fresh perspective on the question I raised and I would like to think about it. Where can I write to you in India?'

Babu: 'Gautam, I am a wanderer, I don't have a fixed address in India. But you can write to me care of Sri Ramanashramam, Tiruvannamalai, Tamil Nadu, India, and your letters will find their way to me, by the grace of Sri Ramana Maharshi.

'Thanks for calling me. Please convey my greetings and gratitude to your parents for their generous hospitality. Bless you! Goodbye, Gautam, goodbye!'

Babu returned the cell phone to George via Muniya, who revealed that the question raised by Gautam had been raised by Indian students at Santa Barbara too, and that she needed to have a fuller discussion with Babu on the matter.

'Hare Krishna!' said George, indicating thereby that Indian spirituality made more sense to him than Indian politics!

At Heathrow Babu and Muniya bade a fond farewell to George.

'I Want To Be Free!'

The Air India flight to Mumbai was delayed (the announcement provided no reasons), and this caused some passengers, fearing terrorist involvement, to cancel their tickets, but Muniya and Babu were undeterred and went through the security check and were happy to wait in the departure lounge for the flight to be announced, strolling up and down aisles between rows of occupied seats until they found a corner where Babu was able to sit down on the floor with his back against the wall (wall and floor make the most comfortable seat, Babu maintained) next to a vacant chair where Muniya sat down.

A transit lounge was symbolically the right place for them to talk about actual transitions which had profoundly changed their lives, and imagined ones which could still do so. But before they could begin an earnest conversation, for which the talkative Babu was much more visibly eager than his rock-sculptured companion, Muniya saw an ISD facility across the hall and decided to call Pune and let Baba and Ayi know that they were on their way home.

'Don't move about suspiciously, Babu, I'll be back in five minutes,' she said. Babu couldn't take his eyes off the all-denim girl with flowing hair (Kali of terminal four, 'denimuniya', he said to himself) who strode across the lounge with determined steps, looking over her shoulders at Babu only once and gesturing with her hand to remind him of her command to stay put until she returned.

She did in five minutes, with Maharashtrian precision, and sat down in her chair next to Babu with an 'This is unbelievable!' expression all over her face.

'Babu, I've just spoken to Baba and he tells me that he and Ayi are in the process of moving to Mumbai, not just to meet us at the airport, but to live in the big city for a few years! Baba has been invited by Air India to Mumbai as a consultant.

'And you know what, Babu! Air India have offered Baba a four-bedroom flat on Marine Drive with a magnificent view of the sea! In the heart of the city where all the action is. Babu, I am excited!' A breathless Muniya reported this at telegraphic speed to a hugely delighted Babu. ('He is not jealous or envious, he is different, my Babu,' she thought to herself, without giving expression to this thought in words, as she had decided not to 'raise hopes and expectations' in Professor Ravi Srivastava's love-crazed heart.)

'And are Baba and Ayi well, and what news of Abhinava?' Babu asked.

'They are, and Abhinava is arriving tomorrow from Delhi to be with all of us. By the way, I let Baba know that I haven't graduated yet, so you are released from the promise of secrecy regarding this matter,' Muniya said.

'Baba wants you to spend a few days at least with us and come up with some design ideas for the house. Babu, surely you will do that, won't you?'

'Why, yes, of course I will, sweetheart, I will spend some time with all of you in your new sea house,' Babu reassured an anxious Muniya.

Dreaming of the new house, Muniya asked Babu what painting he could think of for the living room wall, something indicative of a new phase of life, a turning point, perhaps. She was a student of art herself, and joined Babu in mentally scanning great modern paintings they could remember.

And they held hands, unselfconsciously and unpresumingly, in a spirit of comradeship in this task of divination.

'Muniya, meri duniya, I know just the picture the wall needs. Chagall's "Birthday",' Babu proclaimed, but he saw that she hadn't recalled the picture, and offered a reading of it:

'A woman standing near an open window of her house, already slightly "airborne", but more like a fish than a bird, holds a bouquet of flowers in her hand. Entering the window from the sky outside, upside-down, topsy-turvy in love, is a young man, sliding towards the young woman, the two forming an arc of unspeakable beauty, denying gravity, defying the world!

'Birthday. What is born, awakened, in their hearts, and in the hearts of all viewers of the painting, is the possibility of love being victorious against all odds.'

Babu's voice trailed off at this point. Muniya withdrew her hand from his and covered her face and cried softly and spelt out words of compassion and confession.

'Babu, dearest Babu, you can't be that flying visitor from the sky, I am sorry! Not because in Chagall's painting he is a young man, and you are not.

'Babu, I can sense the depth of your love for me, the unconventional courage and honesty of it. But it is not for want of courage or out of fear of censure that I am unable to reciprocate your love, not even because of any sense of absent chemistry, no!'

'Babu, you are an independent philosopher, a deeply believing, inquiring, Hindu, but not a carbon copy of anybody I can think of.'

'I want to be like you in freedom, and in faith, but I don't want to be a carbon copy even of you or Baba or Ayi....

'Babu, I want to be free but ... I do, I really do love you in my own way, you mean a lot to me ....'

After delivering these words from the depth of her truth-honouring heart, Muniya uncovered her face and found

Babu imitating her smile, implying that she had been imprinted on his soul forever, that he would never be without her, but that he perfectly understood and respected what she was saying.

As they settled into their seats on the aircraft, Babu taking the window seat, Muniya the middle seat, and this time without the aisle seat being vacant, Babu asked her in all seriousness not to forget to ask him all the questions she might still want him to answer to help her in the upcoming viva in a few months.

And that she should do this soon. Because he might not be able to stay with her and Arun and Archana and Abhinava in Mumbai for more than a day or two.

'Why, Babu, where do you have to go? Are you angry with me?' Muniya demanded to know.'

'Pyari. pagli gudiya, how can I be angry with my Guru's deepest gift of understanding to me, which is you?'

'I have to go to Alandi to pray for your happiness, and then to Tiruvannamalai, to pray for myself.'

The big jet was circling over Mumbai, and began its descent. From fantasy to reality.

Grounded In Mumbai

The drive from Chhatrapati Shivaji airport to Marine Drive in Arun's Toyota (the old Ford had to be junked) was arduous and seemingly endless (Mumbai is a straight line, there is not much left or right to the city, Babu thought aloud), enlivened though the journey was by Muniya's entertaining recollections of the days spent in London at the Desai home and the hilarious moments during Babu's lecture at the Bharatiya Vidya Bhavan, especially the interventions of Dr Shrinivas Patwardhan and the frail but fanatical pacifist Englishwoman.

Andheri, Bandra, Mahim, Worli, Mahalakshmi, Pedder Road, Chowpatty, that's the route Arun followed, and at last the new Marine Drive home of the Kulkarnis swung into view, but there was a little problem to be overcome.

The main lift of the apartment building had suddenly stopped working, although the service lift was functioning and Kalpana (Babu was happy to see her after years, older, but still not old) carried Babu's and Muniya's baggage in it to its fourth floor destination. But the service lift refused to come down, and Arun and Babu began their slow ascent of the building's stairway.

Not Muniya, she ran up the stairs like a squirrel, anxious to see her Ayi after her last visit home from Santa Barbara two years earlier. Breathless, she touched her mother's feet, and Archana embraced her luminous daughter and led her into the new but sparsely and functionally furnished home, as the process of shifting from Pune to Mumbai was going to take a while.

Muniya was relieved to learn from her mother that the Pune home was not going to be sold, but in all likelihood rented out to some old friends of Baba's from the Air Force. Abhinava was to arrive later in the evening from Delhi. This was the year he would graduate from St Stephen's. He had been paying more attention to cricket than English literature, but Baba was pleased with his prowess as a leg-break-googly bowler, in Babu's tradition, not Baba's, who had been an opening batsman.

'What does Babu look like now?' Archana asked Muniya, as she showed her around the house. Muniya seemed strangely unwilling to answer that question immediately, choosing instead to reflect on which of the three bedrooms, other than the main bedroom of her parents, she should claim, and which might be more suitable for Abhinava.

'You can decide that later, when Abhinava is also here, but how is Babu, does he look much older than when we last saw him in Pune ages ago?' she asked again.

Muniya walked up to the large window in the dining room which unveiled a heaving, neighbourly, sea, and said, 'Babu is rather like that sea now, grey, disciplined, but troubled,' and quickly added, 'Troubled about the present self-understanding of Hinduism and India,' banishing from her mind other dimensions of Babu's troubled heart which he had revealed to her recently.

'The lifts have struck work and Babu and Baba are climbing the four flights of steps more contemplatively than energetically,' Muniya explained to Archana. This gave Kalpana time to have hot tea ready to serve the mountaineers when they reached the summit. Sitting on the top step of the second floor, Ravi and Arun were catching up on sixteen years of mutual invisibility, although they had corresponded from time to time and spoken to each other on the telephone.

'I can see that your sadhana has slowed the ageing process,' Arun suggested encouragingly.

'Perhaps, but not the worrying process.' Babu answered, and the two friends reflected with sadness on the failure of Indian politics to measure up to the standards of Indian spirituality, the unresolved tensions between India and Pakistan, Hindus and Muslims, and the new world situation of danger after 9/11.

'Arun, do you remember what your college cricket guru, Bose Saheb, had said when, I had, boasting my elementary scientific knowledge, proclaimed that science had proved beyond all doubt that the moon, far from being the romantic sphere of snow that it seems, is hard rock?'

'What did he say, Ravi, I can't recall,' Arun confessed.

'I wouldn't be so sure, I wouldn't be so sure,' he had said, raising the hope that what looks like hard, unalterable, otherness, might be a variant, though deeply camouflaged, form of selfhood, an image of ourselves, Babu recalled, causing Arun immediately to remember Bose Saheb's deceptively simple words.

'Arun, I still cling to that hope,' said Babu, and the duo resumed their trek with greater determination and were glad to be home sooner than they thought it would take.

'Archana!' Babu exclaimed in joy as he embraced his dear friend's wife, and beloved Muniya's mother.

'You have come home again, Babu, to your own home,' Archana declared.

Muniya, standing at the sea window, turned round and caught Babu's eye, and wondered what Babu would say.

'Archana, I have brought Muniya home. But I don't know if, for me, home is Aum, or Aum is home. My spiritual journey is far from complete. I have much wandering to do still. I must go to Alandi to thank Jnaneshvara Maharaj for the blessing of Muniya's companionship during the last few days and to pray for her success in the viva which she must face again soon.'

'And then I must go back to Tiruvannamalai and lay my weary head at the feet of my Master.'

'Babu, your tea is getting cold, and Kalpana has made some uppama just for you!' Muniya said.

Muniya's Light

As Babu lay himself down on the floor of a Marine Drive puja room in Mumbai that night on a cotton mattress covered with khadi sheets, a folded sheet in place of a pillow and a couple of thin shawls placed at the foot of the mattress, he was overwhelmed with gratitude, because that is how Archana used to make his bed in Pune.

'Ramana Maharshi, vibrant in his photograph on one wall, and the ancestral, no less animated, Ganapati on the floor against the opposite wall, sons of Shiva and Parvati, would be ideal companions on a flight to the other world if I were to die tonight,' thought Babu, as he drifted into sleep.

But he was not destined to disappear like a Devadas in a Bombay film. His heart, desperate not to lose Muniya, composed a complex cinematic dream which was unlikely to win any filmfare award, but it brought light into the darkness of his mind.

Babu was flying in his dream, not in an aeroplane, but in a cloud of consciousness.

Timelessly, quickly. He was soon face-to-face with a closed brightly painted green door of a slum house in what he knew with absolute certainty had to be Alandi.

The home of the scavenger woman, Jnaneshvari, as he thought of her, whose darshana he had been blessed with from his bus window on his return journey from Alandi to Pune in 1984. The elegant young woman with a wide forehead, like Muniya's, with her face covered by a dupatta as she swept the ground in front of the chai shack where he had had been engaged in an animated argument with two angry men, possibly neo-Buddhist Dalits, her baby strapped to her back.

As his bus roared away, she had removed her dupatta and revealed her Muniya smile, a sudden widening of eyes and simultaneous rightward shift of her closed mouth.

Closing his eyes and offering her his namaskara, Babu had wondered if she was Muniya's future, adult, form, Jnaneshvari's reminder to him that his beloved feminine form could also be that of a deprived woman. And he knew now that this was so.

The green door opened noiselessly (it was a silent film-dream) and Jnaneshvari stepped out with open arms and smiled at Babu, inviting him not only into her home but also her life.

She was older than when he last saw her, many years older than Muniya, but agelessly his gilehri gudiya.

Anointed with the sacred sweat of scavenging bhakti.

'Will you be mine, Jnaneshvari-Muniya, you are my Muniya in another place, she is you, many-centred?

'Will you let me serve you and love you till my dying day?' Babu pleaded in his heart.

Then two rough men came out of the darkened house, the same men Babu had had an argument with in the chai shack, and they pulled Modigliani-Muniya back into the house. She allowed her arms to fall down in a gesture of helplessness, without withdrawing the blessing of her Atman-smile (the joy of identifying the seat of self on the right side of the chest where there is nothing, Muniya's trademark Advaitin-Buddhist initiation of all into the heart of reality).

'Muniya come back to me, gilehri come back!' Babu shouted,

but the film was gone, the theatre was the puja room, his seat the floor mattress, and Muniya, Ananya Kulkarni, had rushed to his side, hearing his dream scream.

Babu was sweating profusely.

'You'll be all right Babu, you'll be just fine!' said unflappable Muniya.

She was pressing his forehead as she used to in Pune as a child, but with long, strong, hands, not baby palms.

'What happened, Babu?' she asked.

'Nothing, babygirl, I lost a dream to a nightmare.'

'Go back to sleep!'

'No, Muniya, I must wake up now.'

Jnaneshvari's Consolation

Looking at one's reflection in a mirror is a profoundly spiritual experience, and not merely the narcissistic indulgence we allow it to become.

Yes, it tends to feed our sense that we are only a given bodily form; and in its obedient replication of our movements, our mirror image flatters our sense of control over our bodies, with the exaggeration characteristic of all flattery.

But the left-right inversion displayed in our mirror reflection brings an unexpected dimension of non-dualist understanding to the seemingly innocuous experience.

Standing before the mirror image of our bodily forms, our left limbs corresponding to its right ones, we have a sense of our body having 'doubled', turned around and come face to face with itself: a lucid imaging of self-awareness and an intimation that our bodies are self-images of selfhood. A complete Upanishad of everyday life.

It was with a keen sense of the mirror as guru that Babu stood in front of one that morning to shave, and asked the mirror as much as himself what the disturbing Alandi dream might mean.

Without any alteration in the routine movements of the shaving razor, Babu realised that the scavenger woman of his dream, the

Muniya look-alike whom he had seen in the flesh twenty years earlier, was her 'present' form, not a memory, merely.

Babu had to confess to himself that he was hoping to find her again in Alandi, unattached, and offer to be her servant and spouse or lover, forever, as he believed her to be Muniya herself in another place, and without the generation gap that separated him from her California-Pune, graduate-student, incarnation.

It also dawned on Babu that Alandi's Jnaneshvari Muniya was communicating to him through his vivid dream her openness to his love, but her unavailability, the bitter truth that Dalit women could no longer be presumed to be willing and able to accept the love of caste-privileged men.

Circumstances had forced many Dalits to renounce Hinduism, and the Buddhism they wished to embrace would prohibit intimacy between Dalit women and Hindu men. The dream image of Jnaneshvari being pulled away from Babu by angry Dalit men was a retributive mirror-inversion of the strong arm of Hindu orthodoxy prohibiting caste-privileged women from accepting the love of Dalit men.

Babu's love for Muniya had its origins in the realisation twenty years earlier, when he came to Pune to stay with his friend Arun and his family, that there was a fundamental contradiction between Advaita Vedanta's celebration of Atman, self, as ultimate reality, and the miserable state of the girl-child in India throughout her life, despite her being the most lucid self-image of the self-certitude of Atman, the certitude of our existence.

Alandi's Jnaneshvari was urging Babu to return to Tiruvannamalai and Madurai and deepen his understanding of Ramana Maharshi's teaching and its bearing on the condition of the girl-child in India, so that he could serve her cause better.

'Let your beloved Muniya flower in her own way, serve and love her unselfishly through greater resolution in your sadhana of self-realisation,' that is what the Alandi dream was saying.

Babu's astral pilgrimage to Alandi made it unnecessary to repeat it physically.

Roles Reversed!

Breakfast became a viva-voce examination of Babu. Muniya had been explaining to Abhinava the central theme of Babu's recent conversations with her, namely, that the girl-child was the perfect picture of Atman, our deepest reality, self, with some assistance from Arun and Archana who had heard Babu express the same conviction twenty years earlier in Pune.

'Why not the boy-child also?' Abhinava asked Babu, in a slightly hurt and dismissive tone of voice which conveyed a sense that the male gender was being discriminated against in that metaphysical hypothesis, and that this was ground enough for its rejection.

Arun and Archana looked at each other anxiously, thinking that Babu would regard Abhinava's head-on, undergraduate, disagreement as discourtesy, but not Muniya, who looked at Babu amusedly and made a gesture with her hands which seemed to say: 'Babu, the ball is in your court.'

Babu mulled over the query for a whole minute, thus acknowledging the seriousness of the question, and spoke quietly, looking all the while at Abhinava, the spirited young man who was but a baby boy when he last saw him.

'My dear Abhinava, a girl-child, the composite form of childhood and femininity, is the most luminous portrait of self-awareness, self-certainty.

'The special place in our hearts which we accord to our mothers in India is possibly based on an implicit understanding of this philosophical consideration. But we forget the girl-child that our mothers have been, and do not accord to the girl-child as such, whatever be the stage of her life and place in society, the respect that we owe to her unique, upanishadic, status, as a revealer of the certitude of our existence.

'And Abhinava, why leave the eunuch out of consideration in this discussion? For the eunuch also, self-certainty is imaged perfectly by the condition of feminine childhood, for the eunuch also cannot survive childhood without the care, however minimal, of a mother.

'Abhinava, I have never failed to learn something new from a deeply felt, straightforward, philosophical intervention such as yours.

'I can see now, thanks to your interrogation of my conviction, that despite the gender-neutrality of the condition of eunuchhood, the eunuch chooses a female identity, in our country at least, possibly because of the centrality of the form of the girl-child in all self-consciousness, male, female, or eunuch.'

Babu remained lost in that thought for a long time. Awakening Babu from his self-absorption, Abhinava said, 'I must think more about that Babu, but don't forget to send me that print of Ramakrishna Paramahamsa which you promised to last night.' (So Babu had, at dinner, the previous night).

'I will not forget. Ramakrishna in that picture looks like a man, a woman, a eunuch, and above all, he looks like a child, his beard notwithstanding!' Babu exclaimed, and, turning to both Muniya and Abhinava, undiscriminatingly, he asked them if they would like to go to Juhu with him to see his old friend Tyeb Mehta, the great painter.

'Thanks Babu, but I have to go to Matheran with some college friends today, I won't be able to join you,' Abhinava pleaded.

Muniya was excited at the prospect of meeting the painter about whose work Babu had spoken so often and so passionately.

Could Ramakrishna Have Been Gay?

It was years since Babu and Tyeb had spoken to each other last, and when Babu called him from Arun's Marine Drive flat he could barely hear his voice. A mysterious infection (not cancer, mercifully), Tyeb explained hoarsely, had reduced his voice to a whisper, but he said (after a brief word with his wife Sakina) that they would be delighted if Babu and Ananya ('A dear friend's daughter who has just returned from America after a period of graduate study in art and religion,' Babu explained) could join them for tea in their Juhu flat. (Not the old flat, and taking the phone from Tyeb, Sakina gave Babu detailed directions to the new address, which Babu repeated out loud for Muniya to write down, at her insistence!)

Babu and Muniya set off in a taxi after lunch, bumper to bumper with hundreds of other vehicles along the endless stretch of asphalt from Churchgate towards Juhu, both sitting in the back seat (being under no democratic pressure to talk to the driver in India).

Babu was wearing standard white khadi pyjama and kurta and a brown jacket, but Muniya in her rust, mirror-studded, salwar suit and blood red dupatta was a worthy spectacle for a painter of Kali images to behold, Babu thought.

'Muniya, a taxi is a hired vehicle, as I feel my time with you is, hired from destiny which is summoning me to Tiruvannamalai again. I feel we have been given this little space and predetermined time (an hour at least, to get to Tyeb's new home in Juhu) to enable you to ask me the hardest questions you want to, not only to prepare you for your viva, but, babygirl, to prepare me for the lonely life that lies ahead of me, without you,' Babu said, speaking hurriedly as a prisoner would to a visitor with time running out like water in a sink.

Muniya looked anxiously at Babu, and also accusatorily. 'Must you exaggerate? We have lots of time still, your flight to Chennai is scheduled for tomorrow, and you know you will always be there in my prayers and thoughts,' she said, offering a package of consolations which would have been cruel, had they not been sincere, which they were, and had they not brought to her perspiring face (Mumbai is humid) the shimmering authority which the young acquire from truth when they speak the truth, which she did.

'The questions, Muniya, the hard doubts, please, now,' Babu pleaded, his hand reaching out for hers and then withdrawing to fit into the symbolic safety belt which his arms formed around his waist, securing him against possible shocks.

'Very well, Babu,' Muniya began, 'A set of troublesome questions about Ramakrishna and Gandhi, and about you.'

'Shoot, Lakshmibai, I mean, slay!' Babu muttered.

'Muniya drew an imaginary sword from an imaginary scabbard, and sheathed it again, causing both her and Babu to burst into laughter.

'Babu, my dear Babu, why did Ramakrisha caress young boys, even around the genital area, as reported in recent writings on him by western scholars? Is such intimacy compatible with brahmacharya?' Muniya whispered gravely, not wanting the taxi driver to hear what she was saying.

All the rest of the conversation between Babu and Muniya on

Sri Ramakrishna Paramahamsa in sankeertana samadhi

this and related topics was in whispers, unavoidably making Babu think of Tyeb's voice having been reduced to a whisper, as symbolising a needless recourse to confidentiality which would have to characterise all serious conversation in our trivialising or sensationalising age.

'Muniya, meri samajhdar Muniya, listen! Ramakrishna is a self-realised sage, indistinguishable from the Divine Mother, Atman in the ecstasy of its self-imaging art-work.

'His caressing of young boys, all right in the genital area also, merely reveals, and befittingly shockingly to the prurient mind even of our so-called liberated age, the wonder of self-imaging which must characterise the consciousness even of self-realisation. A mother's wonder at the differentiating genitalia of her children, her own variant images: the complementarity, not duality, of their regenerative capabilities.

'Muniya, Ramakrishna's intimacy with the physical forms of some of his spiritual children has the charm of a mother's innocent caressing, washing, of her infants, not the intrusiveness of violative sexuality.

'And in this maternal freedom from fear, Ramakrishna destroys the age-old abhorrence of the body which has distorted spiritual traditions, without licensing any mere indulgence of the body, either.'

'Just as, in his spirited engagement in philosophical argumentation (a whole book needs to be written, Muniya, a book on the mind, not merely the heart, of Ramakrishna), Ramakrishna undermines the rigid reluctance of metaphysical traditions to engage in a playful exploration of their ideas.

'Meri Muniya, Ramakrishna's caressing love of some of his disciples never became sexual indulgence, it remained the unbelieving self-wonder of the divine sculptress beholding her craft.

'Yes, it is often appropriate to speak of Ramakrishna in the feminine mode, so indistinguishable was he in his self-understanding from his mother Kali. A mother's wonder at the apparent difference between her genital form and that of her male progeny, representing the wonder which characterises our, self's, perception of the world as "apparent" not-self. That is what your western investigators of Ramakrishna's inquiring brahmacharya do not understand!' Babu shouted, in so far as it is possible to do so whisperingly.

A long traffic-light halt enabled Muniya to fish out a little notebook and pen from her black jute handbag and write down some hurried notes on all that whispered wisdom of a would-be lover who was also a would-be brahmachari.

'All right Babu, that'll do for the moment on Ramakrishna. Gandhi and you must wait for our return journey,' Muniya said laughingly. But Babu was suddenly very serious.

'Muniya, my hands would dearly caress your form, but they are without the purity of Ramakrishna's heart,' Babu confessed, and closed his eyes, not to hide his tears which flowed unstoppably, but to behold Muniya with his inner eye.

A Falling Figure

It took their taxi driver's vigorous Mumbaiyya speech capabilities to elicit from a sleepy, reluctant, ironing-stall owner the final topographical instructions without which the Lokhandwala Complex, Tyeb's new Juhu residential block, would have remained undiscovered by Babu and Muniya.

Tyeb welcomed Babu and Muniya with a barely audible 'Namaste, Ravi, and Ananya, sit down somewhere, Sakina is in the kitchen, she'll soon serve us the dhoklas which she remembers you liked very much when you visited us in Shantiniketan, Ravi, and we'll drink some elaichi chai, if you are not allergic to it, Ananya?'

'I love elaichi chai and dhoklas, Tyebji,' Muniya said reassuringly and sat down cross-legged on the floor, Babu choosing a hard wooden chair against a wall. Tyeb lowered himself with some difficulty into a comfortable reclining chair facing them, next to a large bookshelf.

'Ananya, Ravi mentioned on the phone that you have studied art and religion somewhere in America ... Santa Barbara, is it?... Well, feel free to look at the books on this shelf, there are not many on religion, but some of the art books which I bought in London ages ago, and which are hard to find now, are there, all over the place, they might interest you ....'

Tyeb's face was wreathed in parental smiles as he spoke these words in his whispering but warm, Gujarati voice.

Touched by the immediacy and generosity of this invitation, Muniya sprang like a gilehri to the bookshelf and busied herself with its nourishing contents.

Babu and Tyeb ruminated about the past and worried about the future of India and the world, wondering if freedom and faith, modernity and tradition, religion and secularism, were ever likely to come together in a spirit of inquiry and humility in the service of all existence, or whether they were doomed to collide like the aeroplanes of terror and the towers of greed did on 9/11, and bring the drama of life and civilisation on earth to an end in the not-too-distant future.

Precisely at this moment of anguish which Tyeb and Babu shared in helplessness, Sakina emerged from the kitchen carrying dhoklas on a tray, and Muniya came running to Babu with a treasure from Tyeb's bookshelf, a book of Chagall prints opened at the page where 'Birthday', the painting Babu had described to Muniya at Heathrow airport, was reproduced: the sailing into one another of an earth-bound bride bearing a bouquet and longing to be airborne, and a flying bridegroom longing for the stability of a grounded home, the gift of an 'open window', open hearts and minds.

The synchronicity of the arrival of Sakina with the dhoklas and Muniya with the reassuring Chagall picture lifted everybody's spirits and the miraculous gifts of home and art were victorious over anxiety, at least temporarily, and tea and dhoklas were partaken of guiltlessly.

The fearlessly truth-inquiring painter could not, however, conceal from Babu and Muniya that he had just recently completed a canvas, 'A Falling Figure', which was not very optimistic about the chances of light, life and truth in the midst of darkness, death and untruth.

Muniya had come across the Gandhi quotation alluded to by Tyeb in that statement during her study of modern religious

The Falling Figure with Bird, Tyeb Mehta, 2003, Acrylic on Canvas, 183 x 140 cm

thinkers at Santa Barbara ('In the midst of death life persists, in the midst of untruth truth persists, in the midst of darkness light persists,' Gandhi had written somewhere), and begged Tyeb to let her (and Babu) see the work not only with the enthusiasm of a graduate student, which would not have impressed Tyeb very much, but also with all the courage of young life wanting to confront truth, however bitter it might be, which touched the painter, and he led Babu and Muniya into his studio to look at the large canvas which showed, frozen in mid-air, a figure which was half-vulture and half-human, the two halves eating into each other's intestines, causing composite life thereby to lose the ability to fly and the ability to walk.

Babu couldn't take his eyes off the painting, and Muniya couldn't take her eyes off Babu's anguished face. Tyeb and Sakina left them alone in the studio.

'What does this awesome work say to you, Babu?' asked Muniya. Babu was speechless for a long time. And then he spoke.

'Everything, I think, that we have been talking about. And more.

'The idea that we, human beings, are nothing but given bodies, destined to perish. So why not perish now?

'The idea that human beings are not any sort of body at all, but a non-physical soul whose true home is heaven. Why not hasten there now?

'These two ideas lie at the back of secular and religious fanaticism.

'Distorting the deliverance of self-awareness that we are all forms, including nothingness, and capable of loving all as ourselves, as Atman.

'Thus distorted, as suggested by the traumatised faces of the vulture and the human being in the painting, secularism and religion are paradoxically not at war with each other, contrary to appearance; but in collaboration, unconsciously, to end the story of life on earth, the lila of the joyous togetherness of diverse forms of self, ourselves and nothingness.

'The painting dramatises the violence of this collaboration. Unmasking terrorism and counter-terrorism.

'The simultaneous destruction of grateful wings and caring feet. 'A fall, surely.

'I think that's what the painting is saying, at least that.

'Chagall's lovers in "Birthday" acquire a new meaning in the light of Tyeb's stark work,' Babu concluded, and looked at Muniya wordlessly and they hugged each other as members of the threatened species called life.

The Ocean's Invitation

Walking barefoot on the sands of Juhu (they had left their footwear in the taxi whose friendly driver had agreed to wait for them and drive them back to Marine Drive), Babu and Muniya were visited by waves upon waves of sea which encircled their feet unsteadyingly. Babu clung to Muniya for support.

'You are not about to be swallowed up by the earth, Babu,' she laughed, and held Babu's hand firmly, her gaze fixed on the horizon which blocked her vision, symbolically, of what the future held in store for her.

Babu felt the sands of time were running out on him. He had failed to win love or liberation, and his thoughts turned to a friend, a practised swimmer, who some years earlier had swum far out into the sea off the Adyar coast in Chennai and was never found again. An ecologically sensitive scientist who had run foul of the scientific establishment of modern India. Many, including Babu, felt he had preferred to surrender to a worthier adversary than iniquitous human life.

'Why can't I do the same?' Babu wondered, and released Muniya's arm from his self-steadying hand-grip.

But he was rudely awakened from his self-centred brooding as Muniya ran far into the water.

'Come back Muniya!' Babu shouted. 'I know you are an expert swimmer, but these sands are treacherous.'

'I'll be all right, Babu, you take care of yourself!' Muniya shouted back.

Babu remembered with embarrassment that he was no swimmer at all, and that drowning in shallow waters would be ignoble and brushed aside the thought of suicide which the remembrance of his friend had stirred in him.

Besides, he saw the half-truth in his despairing thought that he had won neither love nor liberation. True, he had not met any woman who had the luminosity of Muniya, but could her presence in his life be the gift of anything but love?

And had not this gift of love and light unravelled for him the meaning of the lives of the sages of modern India in a way which even prolonged study and meditation had not? Was this gift of understanding not a promise of liberation, moksha?

Babu set aside caution and ran down the sands and joined Muniya, once again holding her arm, not despairingly but gratefully.

'Bravo!' said Muniya, and resumed her interrogation of Indian spiritual and philosophical matters.

'Why is it, Babu, that until fairly recently in historical terms, it was considered evil by Hindu orthodoxy for Hindus to cross the seas? Wouldn't it have been disastrous for India and Hinduism and the world if a Vivekananda or a Gandhi or an Aurobindo, or even you, had been deterred by this prohibition from exploring the wider world and the state and fate of India with the special urgency and insightfulness which unfamiliar surroundings provoke and promote?' Muniya asked, adding, laughingly, 'God! That sounds like you, but believe me, the question has worried me for years.'

'You sound like yourself, sweetheart, don't worry, I wish I could sound like you!'

'But let me offer you an answer to that question which is not based on historical or textual investigation, but which I feel is implicit in the Hindu idea that the supreme goal of life is to realise one's indistinguishability from limitless consciousness, in the way in which all rivers realise their indistinguishability from the ocean by flowing into it and merging with it,' Babu reflected.

'Muniya, the orthodox Hindu prohibition against crossing seas makes profound metaphorical, but no literal, sense. To get from one shore of the sea to another, one world to another, one life to another, is not to become the ocean, the consciousness, the vastness, the emptiness, which images itself as all shores, worlds, lives.

'If we remember this deeper meaning of the ocean, which we are and do not have to cross, the metaphorical meaning of the old prohibition becomes intelligible. That meaning encourages us to seek the limitless, and not merely the multiple forms, however dazzling, of the limited alone.

'Ayi has spoken to me of your swimming prowess, your tireless traversal of several lengths of a swimming pool, and then the effortlessness with which you step out of the pool and with a shake of your head (yes, yes, I am seeing some of this with my inner eye and not repeating Ayi's words) you become dry again like a lotus leaf, self's unaffected, but not unaffecting, immersion in the mire of lives and worlds.'

It was late afternoon, and the sky, which had been unusually clear for Mumbai in September, suddenly started to darken with a mass of clouds billowing above the sea.

A strong wind caused the clouds to collapse into one another and weave out of their dark fabric an ominous shape.

A mighty falling, slowly disintegrating figure, agonised vulture and unyielding man, eating into each others vitals: Tyeb's falling figure which they had seen only an hour earlier.

Was this sky-art or a Hiroshima mushroom formation prophesying apocalypse? Or projection?

'Let's go home, Babu,' said Muniya.

Babu had not heard a sweeter summon than that in all his life.

Hindutva or Sindhutva?

It was early evening when Babu and Muniya began their return journey to Marine Drive. Groups of demonstrators belonging to an extremist Hindu organisation were trying to block traffic all along the way in protest against an armed attack that had been launched earlier in the day in Delhi on the Lok Sabha building by armed terrorists purportedly supported by Pakistan. Any Muslim would have been the target of the fury of protesters.

The taxi radio gave details of what had happened, the shooting down of security guards and all the terrorists, a narrow escape for members of parliament, including the Prime Minister and the leader of the opposition, who had gathered to conduct the business of Indian democracy.

Babu was furious too, though he was strongly opposed to retaliatory action of any kind against Indian Muslims who could have had nothing to do with the attack.

He believed that with all its imperfections, the Indian Parliament was a unique institution in the world, not only because it represented nearly a billion people belonging to all faiths and none, including also the non-human inhabitants of India who were objects of special adoration and worship for the vast constituencies of adivasi members of the Parliament, and also millions of Hindus: the unique, non-anthropocentric representativeness of the Indian Parliament was sacred to Babu, the round shape of the Lok Sabha building suggestive of the vast possibilities of transformation of human consciousness towards self-realisation with which Indian democracy in its spiritual comprehensiveness was pregnant.

The attack on the Lok Sabha symbolised the envy of comprehensive India nursed by secessionist, hegemonist, narrowness, Babu felt, and gave animated voice and words to all these hurt sentiments, addressing both Muniya and the taxi driver and God.

At the same time, Babu expressed great sorrow that Hindu politics was destroying the openness of Hindu thought by imitating the sectarian narrowness of Islamic orthodoxy in Pakistan.

The taxi driver had little time to enter into any discussion with Babu on all these matters as he was skilfully, but with great difficulty, avoiding all areas of disruption and conflagration and hurrying his vehicle and his passengers along narrow lanes known only to his breed of charioteers, and heading heroically towards the Churchgate area.

Predictably, Muniya did not interrupt Babu's soliloquy, and only when he fell back exhausted on the steeply slanted back of the taxi seat and winced in rheumatic pain, did she open her mouth, and asked Babu to define Hinduism, and to distinguish it, if this was possible, from 'Hindutva', the variation favoured by extremist Hindu organisations.

Babu realised he had been in free flow for a long time, and after several minutes of prayerful silence, he spoke again.

'"Hindu", as we know, is a colloquially modified form of the Sanskrit word "Sindhu", a word which, dear girl, means "a river", the river Sindhu, Indus, which has generated the name "India". But, and this is less widely known, the word "Sindhu" also means sea, of which we have recently had a darshana.

'The word which would identify the deepest faith of the followers of Hindu spirituality is not the uninspired English word

"Hinduism", which reduces an unbroken tradition of realisation to an "ism", an ideology, nor the hybridised construction "Hindutva", which means exactly what "Hinduism" does, glorying vainly in the Sanskrit suffix "tva".

'The word we need is "Sindhutva" or "Sindhuism", to acknowledge the central current of Hindu spirituality, the flow of a river towards the sea, nourishing all the land and life along the way, and the return of the sea as rain to form rivers which seek the sea again and again.

'Babygirl, this is not just a linguistic matter. "Hinduism" and "Hindus" suggest inevitably, as would "Hindutva" and "Hindutvavadis", a matter of counting heads, a census exercise, a slide towards anthropocentric majoritarianism and minoritarianism which has ripped India apart; India, the trustee of the mystical identity of the apparently finite and limited with the infinitude of limitless consciousness, the river and the sea.

'India's other name, "Bharata", as a sannyasin once explained to me, does not mean "the land of the descendants of King Bharata", a terribly limited, anthropocentric, potentially racist, meaning, but "light-obsessed", "illumined" as is suggested by the root "bha", suggestive of light as in the names "Abha", "Vibha", "Bhaskara", and so on.

'Muniya meri, the answer to the insipidity of "Hinduism", the cultural absentmindedness of "secularism", and the delusionary reductionism of "Hindutva" is "Sindhutva", "Sindhuism".

'I hope your generation of Indians, of all faiths and none, will one day uphold the trustee spirit of "Sindhutva" and save India and the world from annihilationist, numericalist, anthropocentrism.'

Thus concluded Professor Ravi Srivastava's lecture, and the conclusion was greeted with relief (and gratitude) by Muniya's mock-mock clapping. But Babu was not done yet.

'Muniya, it was the devastation of the Sindhutva possibilities of Indian unity by its cynical dismemberment which prompted Gandhi's concluding brahmacharya experiments in Noakhali, when he and some of his women associates slept side by side in their birthday suits at night, not sexually covetously, but in a defiant, gender-transcending, gesture of non-duality. And in vulnerable identification with the hundreds of thousands of women who were raped and killed by men crazed by dualistic delusions of separateness and vengefulness.'

'I must think more about that, dear Babu.

'You haven't noticed, but we are in the Victoria Terminus area and will soon be home, thanks to our ingenious charioteer.'

'What's your name, dear friend?' Babu asked the taxi driver as he paid him his fare.

'Krishnayya, Sir!' the man replied, shyly.

'Krishna, always the charioteer,' thought Babu.

'How tired are you, Babu?' asked Muniya, as they were about to take the lift to the fourth floor.

'I am not tired at all, let's walk up the steps, slowly, and talk some more. But I am going to hold the banister and you are going to hold my arm, Muniya!' Babu insisted.

'Done!' was Muniya's response.

'Babu, my examiners did not ask me any questions on art, but they might this time. There is a question my art tutor had asked me about Van Gogh's "Crows in the Wheatfields", you know the ominous work which many regard as Vincent's "suicide note". Is the painting really that? Is there not a more universal meaning to it? That's the question my tutor had asked. I wonder if you have any thoughts on the subject?' Muniya asked Babu with the earnestness of a graduate student which was nevertheless charged with the anxiety of life uncertain about its future.

As the two inquirers wound their way up the steep staircase, Babu saw the painting in his mind as though for the first time. And sat down on the top step of the first floor, and spoke to Muniya with closed eyes. Anxious not to lose what was becoming apparent to him.

'Muniya rani, the tangled gold of the wheatfield is the rich but abused wealth of the earth, demanding from us the response of a "middle path" of ethical and ecological responsibility, not the extreme paths of consumerism and control which in the painting lead nowhere.

'But the crows are aeroplanes of vengeance and counter-vengeance, a rainfall of bombs, and if you look carefully at the middle path which seeks desperately to wind its way across the field, it suddenly closes.

'The dualisms of heaven and earth, religion and science, East and West, seem to have closed the middle path of wisdom for humanity.

'The painting is a warning or a prophecy of disaster, meri pyari Muniya! '

Babu's eyes had filled with tears and Muniya removed his spectacles and wiped their lenses with her dupatta, but she was deeply troubled too.

'Babu, tell me truthfully, is there hope? Hope for me? Will I find home, rest, freedom, community, love?'

Muniya's anguish caused Babu to think of Andrew Wyeth's 'Christina's World', and he asked Muniya if she knew the work. She did, vaguely.

'Muniya, there is hope. Look at Christina in the picture. She is sprawled on a field, not unlike the field in Van Gogh's catastrophic vision.

'And look, look, babygirl (Babu's eyes were still closed), Christina is crippled, like life today, like the girl-child, like childhood, like self-awareness.

'But there at the edge of the field is her home, and she is crawling courageously towards it. She will get there, Muniya!' Babu affirmed with prophetic optimism and a choked voice.

When they were on their feet again, Babu saw Muniya suddenly like the waitress in Manet's 'A Bar at the Folies-Bergere'.

Alone, with life's gifts of flowers and fruits and wine all around her, her offerings to the world which fails to see her as the finest image of its inmost reality, self, and seeks instead to look at its egoistic forms in the mirror behind her.

Edouard Manet (1832-1883): A Bar at the Folies-Bergère, 1882, Oil on Canvas, 96x130 cm

Samadhi

The long and talkative visit to Juhu with its excitement and anguish extracted their price the morning after, when Babu woke up without a voice.

His smiling but silent presence at breakfast was the cause of much amusement and remembrance. Abhinava had returned from Matheran, and talked excitedly about the altitude jogging he and some of his friends had indulged in (he was not, unlike twenty years earlier, in Kalpana's arms, crying), and Muniya spoke to her parents about the sindhutva identity of Indian spirituality with all the excitement of a graduate student waiting to confront detractors and trivialisers of Hinduism and India with the new idea when she returned to Santa Barbara in a couple of months. She was not in mauna, unlike twenty years earlier.

Babu was, with Muniya's initiatory smile imprinted on his face, as evidence that he was not bereft of the potentiality of speaking, nor of the grace of sages. Arun and Archana and Kalpana, who was serving extra portions of uppama to Babu, burst into simultaneous laughter as the extraordinary inversion of roles which that scene represented dawned on them, and Archana explained the cause of their laughter to their children.

Muniya had of course heard accounts from her parents of her stubborn speechlessness as a child, and Babu's role in her emergence from that condition on her birthday on 2 October 1984, and she consummated the inversion of roles by looking at Babu intently, her initiatory smile glowing, and spoke reassuringly to him:

'Dearest Babu, I know you understand deeply all that we are saying, choosing not to speak as a gesture of solidarity with the aggrieved girl-child in our country, but won't you, my precious babyboy, say "Aum", the source of all speech and silence, not now, necessarily, but whenever the grace of Ramana prompts you to do so, won't you, for Muniya's sake?'

Moved to tears and coughing laughter by this compassionate plea and luminous playacting, Babu excused himself with a gesture suggestive of his need to go to the loo and soon returned to the puja room to sort out his life.

He was flying out to Chennai in the evening, and would hurry from there by taxi to Tiruvannamalai.

It was time to say farewell to Muniya. But was he ready for this separation from the light and love of his life?

Muniya came into the puja room with a big comb and handed it to Babu.

Wordlessly, Ravi Srivastava combed Ananya's long and unruly hair for what seemed like ages. She hummed the tune of his favourite film song: 'Tu jahan jahan chalega, mera saya satha hoga.'

Babu wove Muniya's hair into five long strands, representing the five elements, the five senses, the five Pandavas married to singular-mind Draupadi, all grounded in Muniya's, Krishna smile, self, Atman.

Straining his vocal chords, Babu whispered into both her ears the plea: 'Be mine in another life, Muniya!'

As his plane lifted off into the sky later that evening, Muniya's fearlessly truthful answer to his plea, worthy of her heroic parents, rang in his ears: 'I'll think about that Babu, I will.'

Babu was desperate. He was not yet ready to go farther and farther away from Muniya.

'Appa!' he cried, 'Let me hear Muniya's voice in my heart and feel that she is "with" me, talking to me, teaching me.'

Declining in-flight refreshments, Babu sat up in his seat in the most upright position possible and settled into meditation, and spoke to Muniya.

> Muniya meri, I knew from the time I first saw you in Pune in 1984 that no truth was hidden from you, and just as I was able to cajole you into saying 'Aum' then, I want my meditation to draw from you a story which sums up all that I have been trying to say to you and others about the symbolism of the girl-child. May Ramana help you enlighten me!

And it wasn't long before he began to hear her voice deep within his heart, clear and authoritative. Babu imagined it to be the voice of Minakshi, the fish-eyed Goddess who led Ramana from death to immortality, unreality to reality, darkness to light.

And Muniya-Minakshi's voice told him, with the license of storytelling, the essence of the Kena Upanishad story of the Gods and Brahman and Uma Haimavati.

It went something like this:

> Chin up, Babu, listen to this extraordinary story of the Gods as it is recorded in the Kena Upanishad, and your melancholy will melt away, because the story confirms your hunch about the girl-child being the perfect portrait of Atman.
>
> The Gods had won a battle against the Demons, and were rather puffed up about this victory of theirs and allowed their little light of ego to push the radiance of self-awareness into the background.
>
> Keen to teach the Gods a lesson in humility, Brahman appeared in the garden of Indra's palace at night as a luminous young woman whose light far exceeded the light of Indra, Agni, Vayu, and all the other Gods put together, causing them much jealousy.

Indra sent Agni to find out who this intrusive light was.

'Who are you?' Agni asked her.

'I know who you are,' she said. 'You are Agni, and you think you can burn everything to cinders. Try burning this blade of grass here.'

Agni sizzled with all his might but could not singe the blade of grass.

Indra sent Vayu to investigate the strange light in the midst of the comparative darkness of heaven.

'I know you are Vayu,' the girl said, 'You believe you can blow all things away, deny stability to anything. Try blowing away this blade of grass here.'

Vayu blew himself hoarse but could not move the blade of grass at all.

Indra, mind itself, came out now to interrogate the trespassing girl, but she disappeared into the ether, shining and soaring like a comet. Indra followed her throughout the domain of emptiness, hoping to catch up with her, thinking that she must be something as opposed to something else, but came nowhere close to her. Because she was the light of self-awareness, which imaged itself as all things, and was not any one thing as opposed to other things.

Suddenly Indra found himself on a bare rock of the great Himalaya mountain, which had been virtually denuded by the depredatory greed of humanity.

It was no longer dark and there she was, the luminous girl, standing fearlessly before the greatest of the Gods, her light her smile, a sudden widening of eyes and a simultaneous sideward movement of the mouth.

'I know who you are,' said the girl clad in the tattered clothes of poverty.

'You are Indra, and you have forgotten that the mind, like all things and nothingness, is but a self-image of self-luminous Atman. And powerless without it.

'In forgetfulness of this truth, ego reigns in all worlds. This beautiful earth, teeming with life, can as a result sink into darkness like the light of mind without self-awareness, like you, Indra.

Vishnu offering Minakshi in marriage to Sundareshvara, Madurai

'I am Uma Haimavati, daughter of Himalaya, a girl-child, a young woman, who suffers untold misery because neither humans nor gods nor demons realise that the condition of childhood is the only absolute certainty in experience, the knowledge that we have been children. Along with its unforgettable feminine companion, our mothers.

'The girl-child, in all stages of her life, is the perfect picture of what you have forgotten, the self-luminous reality of selfhood, Atman.

'I manifested in your world to remind you of this truth, and have lured you here, brought mind down to earth, to remind all humanity that in ill-treating the girl-child they ill-treat their deepest reality, Atman, self-awareness.

'Babu, I am Muniya, a girl-child who has enabled you to understand an aspect of your Guru's teaching which can make life worth living for millions of girl children in our country and elsewhere.

'I had read a translation of the Kena Upanishad at Santa Barbara without understanding its meaning at all deeply. You have helped me understand the story of Agni's, Vayu's, and Indra's encounter with the light of Brahman, self-awareness, and you have heard the story in my voice because you and I are one. I am always there for you as you. Chin up, Babu.'

Babu's conversation with Muniya in daharakasha (the space of the heart) continued.

'Thank you, Muniya, but don't go away as yet, the significance of a sacred story has just occurred to me and I want to share it with you. Are you with me?

'Muniya, listen! Minakshi, Madurai's fish-eyed Goddess was born to a Pandyan king and queen who had been childless for many years.

'They brought up the little girl as they would a son, training her in all the arts and sciences, especially the martial arts.

'Minakshi acquired unsurpassed eminence as a warrior while still a young girl.

'She was all of sixteen years old when she conquered all the worlds, Muniya (as you must have when you left Sanawar!), and was about to overwhelm Kailasa, Shiva's abode.

'Shiva saw her riding towards him on a horse, an illumined form like the one whom Indra, Agni and Vayu had encountered in the Kena Upanishad, and he fell instantly in love with her!

'Muniya, Minakshi sensed this, and reciprocated his love with a smile like yours, and decided to return to Madurai.

Shiva followed her all the way back to her parent's palace and asked the Pandyan king for his daughter's hand in marriage.

'Realising that their daughter must be a form of Parvati herself, Minakshi's parent's had no hesitation in accepting Shiva's proposal.

'Their marriage was performed with all beings in attendance under the canopy of nothingness, and its consummation resulted in Minakshi becoming the sacred sculpture in the Madurai temple where she continues to be worshipped as the most perfect image of Atman-Brahman.

'Are you with me, Muniya, Muniya? Where are you? Babu was shouting and found a stewardess looking at him with anxiety.'

'Please fasten your seat-belt, Sir, we shall be landing shortly in Chennai. We have a physician at Chennai airport who can examine you, if you are not feeling well. And if no one is coming to the airport to receive you, is there anyone you would like us to call on your behalf?' the stewardess asked Babu, reassuringly.

'Yes, Dr Ramana Maharshi, but I don't have his Tiruvannamalai phone number.

'You can think of him and he will come to my aid.'

Babu fastened his seat belt, drew up his legs, and closed his eyes. His mouth made a slight rightward movement, and he was absorbed in Ramana.

'Aum Shantih Shantih Shantih.'

Glossary

Advaita Vedanta: Indian philosophical and spiritual tradition of non-duality, which maintains that Atman or self is sole reality.
Alandi: shrine of Sant Jnaneshvara near Pune.
Amarnath: snow-bound shrine of Shiva in Kashmir.
Appa: a Tamil word which means father, the source, ground, of all manifestation, Atman and Brahman.
Arani sticks: sticks by rubbing which fire for sacred rituals is kindled.
Arunachala: sacred hill in Tamil Nadu, South India, regarded as indistinguishable from Shiva.
Arya Samaj: reformist sect of Hinduism founded in the nineteenth century by Svami Dayananda Sarasvati.
Ashvamedha yajna; horse: a sacred ceremony performed by victorious sovereigns in ancient India. The horse which is let loose during the ceremony and returns unharmed, is known as the ashvamedha horse.
Atman: self, not ego, our indubitable reality. Self-awareness.
Aum: most sacred mystic utterance of Hinduism which is regarded as indistinguishable from ultimate reality, Atman and Brahman.
Aum Sri Ramanaya Namah: mantra of obeisance to Sri Ramana.
Ayi: Marathi word for mother.
Ayodhya agitation: a recent Hindu movement which claims that an ancient Rama temple in Ayodhya was demolished at the instance of the Mughal Emperor Babur and a mosque built in its place in the sixteenth century. The mosque was demolished by Hindu zealots in 1992.

Baba: common designation in India for father.

Babu: common affectionate designation in eastern Uttar Pradesh for an elderly man.

Babur: founder of the Mughal Empire in India.

Baby meri, kuch nahin hua hai, mujhe apne dil ki baat bata de: common Hindi words of tender love with the aid of which the hidden and hurtful sadness of a loved one is sought to be alleviated.

Bandgala: collarless, buttoned up jacket, piece of formal modern Indian male attire.

Bhadraloka: a term by which the culturally refined sections of Bengali society are identified.

Bhishma: heroic elder of the Kuru clan who fought on the side of the Kauravas against the Pandavas in the Kurukshetra war, also known as Devavrata.

Brahmacharya: celibacy; more spiritually, as Sri Ramana explains, living in the Vast (Brahman).

Brahman: literally, the Vast. Ultimate reality, identified in Advaita Vedanta with Atman, self.

Brahmarshi: a sage who has realised Brahman.

Cape Comorin: the southern-most tip of the Indian peninsula.

Chal Kalkatta dhar de paise: a refrain which imitates the movement of the steam-driven locomotive, but is also a warning that going to Calcutta (now Kolkata) will deprive you of all your wealth; or, if you are a devotee of Kolkata's presiding deity, Kali, all your ego.

Chatushpat: literally, four-footed, but thereby hangs a theological and sociological tale.

Cobra pigtail: thick pigtail, heavily knotted, favoured by young women and women dancers, strongly suggestive of the unfurled Kundalini Shakti, yogic power, believed by Indian yogic traditions to be dormant at the base of the spine, and capable of raising its hood like a cobra.

Darshana: perceptual encounter, involving eye-contact, with a spiritually realised person or a divine personage, or a deep perceptual encounter with the sacred aspects of nature.

Dharma: all-upholding order of righteousness.

Duniya: world, everything.

Dupatta: long, often intricately embroidered scarf, worn especially by women in North India.

Fourth Varna: the fourth, historically oppressed, shudra, caste of orthodox Hindu social hierarchy.
Gandhara: ancient Indian name for Afghanistan.
Gayatri Mantra: mantra of obeisance to the self-luminous light of Atman symbolised by the light of the sun, believed by Hindus to have been revealed to the sage Vishvamitra.
Gilehri: squirrel, affectionate mode of addressing a zestful, mischievous, beloved, girl.
Gudiya: literally doll, affectionate mode of addressing a beloved girl-child or young girl.
Hare Rama Hare Rama Rama Rama Hare Hare, Hare Krishna Hare Krishna Krishna Krishna Hare Hare: mantra of singing and dancing to the glory of Rama and Krishna, revealed to Chaitanya Mahaprabhu in the sixteenth century, and made popular all over the modern world in the twentieth century by Sri Bhaktivedanta Prabhupada.
Hari, Hari: an invocation of Sri Krishna.
Hastinapur: capital city of the Kuru clan in the Mahabharata.
Hind Svaraj: Mahatma Gandhi's revolutionary tract of 1909 questioning the moral supremacy of modern European civilisation.
ISKCON: International Society for Krishna Consciousness – an organisation founded by Sri Bhaktivedanta Prabhupada in the second half of the twentieth century with centres around the world for propagating devotion to Sri Krishna.
Jai Durge: an invocation of Goddess Durga, and a celebration of her victory over the darkness of ego represented by the demon Mahishasura.
Jai Gopala: a celebratory invocation of Sri Krishna.
Jai Svaraj: an invocation of svaraj, freedom, which also means self-realisation.
Janaka: sage father of Sita.
Jhoola: swing.
Kabaddi: a rural Indian sport of profound spiritual significance.
Kali: all-powerful Divine Mother.
Kaliyuga: the present age of spiritual darkness.
Kanyakumari: Goddess whose shrine at Cape Comorin, especially the single diamond which adorns her image, is regarded as nothing less than the light of India which draws the whole world to it.
Karna: Kunti's first born (eldest of the Pandavas) whom she had

abandoned as a baby, and who grew up to fight on the side of the Kauravas against his own brothers.
Kathavachaka: traditional storyteller of the sacred.
Kayastha: a caste of Hindu administrators.
Kena Upanishad: a text of esoteric instruction which tells of the humbling of gods by the light of Brahman and its unsurpassable feminine form, Uma Haimavati, Parvati.
Khadi thaan: a length of hand-spun cloth.
Kshira Bhavani: shrine of the Divine Mother in Kashmir where Svami Vivekananda heard her voice in 1898, emanating not from her image but from the sky, reminding him that she had protected all faiths in India.
Kuru: all-powerful clan of warriors in the Mahabharata; Kaurava, a member of the clan.
Kurukshetra: battlefield of the Mahabharata war.
Lanka: a word in Sanskrit which means island, or ego, not the state of Sri Lanka.
Lok Sabha: Indian Parliament.
Mahabharata: the work which describes the Mahabharata war and Sri Krishna's role in it, besides being a sourcebook of Indian philosophical wisdom.
Mahasamadhi: the casting away of the physical body by a self-realised sage.
Mahishasura: stubborn illusion, represented by a buffalo-form, slain by Durga, Illumination.
Mala: necklace.
Manduka; Mandukya Upanishad: the sage Manduka, literally a frog, and the Upanishad revealed to him.
Mangalasutra: necklace worn by married Hindu women, literally thread of blessedness.
Maricha: a demon who appears in the guise of a deer to lure Rama and Lakshmana away from Sita to make it possible for Ravana to abduct her. The episode has vast dimensions of meaning.
Marital Garland of Letters: title of a set of devotional poems composed by Sri Ramana Maharshi and addressed to the sacred hill Arunachala, characterised by uninhibited erotic-mystic symbolism.
Maryada Purushottama: a designation of Sri Rama which means Supreme Being who upholds honour.
Maya: the illusion of otherness.

Meri pyari Muniya: My beloved Muniya.
Minakshi: divine daughter of a Pandyan king and queen, near whose temple in Madurai is where the sixteen-year-old boy Ramana attained Moksha.
Moksha: self-realisation.
Mumbaiyya speech: the vibrant colloquial speech of Mumbai residents.
Muniya: a common mode of addressing a girl-child, or a young woman, in eastern Uttar Pradesh; also a name of the Divine Mother conceived as a playful bird who wrecks all our evil plans.
Namaskar; Namaste: greeting, with folded hands, as obeisance to the divine in all.
Neti, Neti: an upanishadic mode of withholding the status of reality from all alleged otherness.
Nirvana: Buddhist enlightenment.
Noakhali: a small district in East Bengal (now Bangladesh), witness to terrible carnage during India's partition, where Gandhi and some of his co-workers, men and women, staked all to save innocent lives and restore communal harmony.
Pandavas: the five heroic brothers in the Mahabharata war who surrendered only to Sri Krishna: Yudhishthira, Bhima, Arjuna, Nakula, Sahadeva.
Parikshita: Arjuna's grandson who was a fatally wounded foetus in his mother Uttara's womb, but who was miraculously saved by Sri Krishna, along with his mother.
Patalalingam: a lightless underground vault in the Arunachaleshvara temple in Tiruvannamalai where Sri Ramana spent weeks in the bliss of self-realisation.
Pauranika: traditional storyteller of the sacred, a genre of such storytelling.
Pondicherry: the town in Tamil Nadu where Sri Aurobindo did his sadhana of integral Yoga.
Porbandar: birth-place of Mahatma Gandhi.
Prajapati: Creator.
Purna: wholeness.
Quit India: the battle-cry of the non-violent movement launched by Gandhi in 1942 demanding the end of British racist rule in India.
Ramakrishna Kathamrita: monumental record of the conversations of Sri

Ramakrishna Paramahamsa, which continues to nourish the soul of modern India.
Ramayana: the epic poem of the drama of the lives of Rama and Sita.
Rani of Jhansi, Jhansi-ki-Rani: the young woman warrior who chose death in battle rather than surrender the sovereignty of her state of Jhansi to the British in 1857.
Rudraksha Mala: a garland made of seeds which represent Shiva's or Rudra's inner or third eye of illumination.
Sadhana: spiritual practice.
Sadhu: exemplar of spiritual and moral integrity, not necessarily a mendicant.
Sadguru: self-realised teacher of self-realisation, Atman itself.
Samadhi: absorption in the divine, death as conceived by devotion.
Sannyasa: renunciation.
Sankeertana: singing and dancing to the glory of God.
Siddhi(s): occult power(s).
Satsanga: communion of spiritual seekers.
Satyagraha: Gandhi's notion of cleaving to truth in all spheres of life, not excluding the political.
Sukhasana: comfortable yogic posture.
Tattvamasi: upanishadic assurance that we are what we seek.
Tatumsi: a child's babbling reiteration of the upanishadic assurance tattvamasi.
Tu jahaan jahaan chalega, mera saya sath hoga: a line of a popular film song which assures the beloved that wherever he may be, her shadow will accompany him.
Tu jiye hazaaron saal, har saal ke din hon pachaas hazaar: wishing someone a long life, metaphorically thousands of years.
Uma Haimavati: daughter of Himalaya, Parvati, the girl-child in the Kena Upanishad who reminds Indra, that is, mind, that his, its, light, is but a reflection of the light of self-awareness.
Vijayadashami: the day which marks the overcoming of illusion, Mahishasura, by illumination, Durga.
Yama: Death.
Yaksha: celestial artist.